Lilli's Story

M. Stephens

For further information, please contact TEL Publishing

terrylursen@gmail.com

Lilli's Story

This is a work of fiction. All of the characters and events portrayed in this book are fictional and any resemblance to real people or incidents is purely coincidental.

Cover Design: Stephen Lursen Art

Editor: Terry E. Lursen

Publisher: TEL Publishing

ISBN: 978-1-970094-01-5 Print paperback

ISBN: 978-1-970094-02-2 ebook

Library of Congress Cataloging-in-Publication Data

Stephens, M., 1947 –

lilli's story

Library of Congress Control Number: 2018915329

"Just remember,

I carry your heart with me,

I carry it in my heart…"

E.E. Cummings

Table of Contents

Lilli's Story

Prologue

The restaurant where they met every Sunday night for the past year was small, dimly lit, and quaint. It was simply decorated with a contemporary flair which was so unusual for an Italian restaurant.

There were no red checkered table cloths or candles being held up by woven straw wine bottles. Soft white tablecloths lay gently across the five rows of tables and six booths that were snuggled tightly in all the corners of this little house. Pale pink napkins stood tall on the charger plates. The walls were a pale grey with swirls of light and dark shades of pinks and burgundy running through it. The chairs were finely upholstered in grey silk fabric. Grey accordion shades and matching valances covered the windows.

They were always the first to arrive in the daylight, so the cylinder-shaped glass oil lamps were never lit. They felt at home as soon as they stepped into this charming house. Lilli felt comfortable here and looked forward to her Sunday dinner each week.

Lilli was always well put together. She wore very little make-up and her hair was always held softly behind her ears with a simple leather headband. She was a realist and knew her years were showing now, and admitted to herself that her body was slightly out of shape. She made sure her clothes fit well and were becoming to a woman of her age. She never wanted to be branded as a cougar or a middle-aged woman in crisis. No animal prints or spiked heels were in her wardrobe. Mary Kay makeup and gaudy jewelry were not her style.

Lilli Belle Jackson knew she was now only a month away from living quite a few years beyond a half century. In her fifty-five years, she was a daughter, wife, mother, grandmother, widow, and now a lover to a much younger man. How did she get here? More importantly, where does she go from here?

Chapter 1

TWO AND A HALF YEARS EARLIER

After the untimely and unexpected death of her beloved husband, Elgin Thomas Jackson III, Lilli was lifted out of her life and world as she had known it for the last thirty-five years.

She experienced an abnormal grieving process that very few people know about or have gone through. She was free falling in and out of every day from all the ties that bound her to her existence. She laid in bed, and hardly blinked her eyes. For hours, her pupils had become fixed on the ceiling fan and her eyes ached. After she cried her tears, she experienced low aching groans that came on without warning.

The shutters were closed as tightly as she had now shut herself off from everyone in her world. The first weeks after Elgin's burial she didn't leave her bed. She barely ate scraps of food and drank water that her daughters had left at her bedside. Most days the trays of food were brought in and out of her bedroom untouched. She tried to explain that she couldn't swallow it. It stopped at her throat. It was physically impossible. Her skin tone had now gone from rosy pink to ashen grey. Her daughters called on Uncle Steve, Elgin's best friend to intervene. He talked to her about the importance of nourishment. He told her that if she didn't start eating something, her daughters would end up losing their mother, too. He said that he had lost patients who gave up on life when their spouses died. He assured her that this could happen if she didn't try to go on with her life for her daughters and six grandkids.

Day after day, her girls would sit on the bed or in the window seat and try to make conversation. They would tell her about what the children said and did and tried desperately to get a reaction. She would half smile at them and then ask them to close the shutters. This was their clue to leave her alone now.

Finally, at the urging of her son-in-law, Dana, a grief counselor was brought in. For the next few weeks, Linda Richards would drop by and talk to Lilli. One day, Lilli got up and left her bedroom. Linda had broken through. Linda was firm with her and told her she had to get up and pull her family back together. She was now the head of the Jackson clan. She had to do this for the sake of her daughters. They too were grieving and would never start to heal because of her intense grief.

Now when her daughters visited, she would come downstairs and sit with them in the kitchen as the kitchen table was where the Jackson family shared many conversations and lots of laughs. It was truly the heart of their home and where they came together every night to share their lives.

As the months ticked by, Lilli's daughters got back into some normalcy of the lives they once knew. They believed their mom would come around soon as well. She did seem better, after all, she now got dressed and would sit in the kitchen with them. What the girls didn't know, was that as soon as they left the driveway, Lilli walked right back into her bedroom and closed the lights and shutters. Elgin's little dog Gigi would jump on the bed and lay close to her. It was touching how Elgin's dog had now become Lilli's constant companion.

She would talk to the dog, "Do you miss him as much as I do?"

As Lilli lay in bed stroking Gigi's soft white fur, she would float away and find herself in the same place, time and time again. She would relive the final moments of Elgin's life. In some strange way it comforted her to hold on to those very sad last minutes with him. It was her last memory of them as a couple. She worried and wondered if her memories were going to be something that she would have to help her get through the days and nights or would they end up being what she would lose as the years went by.

 She would visualize the flashing lights and feel the sirens burning her ears. She could feel him as he was cupped in her arms and saw him slipping further away from her.

"Why did you have to get out of the car? You could have called for police help," she pondered.

The road was so dark as the rain pounded. It was the wettest, darkest, ugliest night she had ever seen.

She should have insisted that he call the police and stay in the car.

Her mind continued, "It was a flat tire, not a car accident. Why did you have to be such a good soul? After all, that's the reason I fell in love with you so many years ago, wasn't it?"

He was such a good man. Not a mean bone in his body. She was angry with herself, angry with him, but really angry that God would take him away from her. If only she had been more forceful insisting that he not get out of the car…if only they had called for help, she wouldn't be sitting here alone with his dog.

"Why God? Why?" She murmured.

She thought for hours on end about the other driver. Hit and run, they call it. She had seen the red car swerve and almost go off the road as it skidded to correct itself. Then she saw Elgin being flung into the heavens like a rag doll. She tried not to relive that image, but it returned to her with an unforgiveable vengeance. The redness of the blood reappears as it flows effortlessly from his nose, mouth and ears.

She repeated her words as he lay dying, "Don't leave me, please, I love you so much. Please God, please someone, help him."

As the ambulance pulled into Summerville General Hospital's emergency lot, she could see Steve waiting there for them. Then, it all slows down as she remembers being ushered into a private family waiting suite. There she made calls to her daughters. She told them that Elgin was in the hospital and Uncle Steve was examining him now. She briefly told them there was an accident, and that he had been struck by a car…out on Hilltop Road. They all said they would be there as soon as possible. The next fifteen minutes ticked by slowly and as Steve emerged in the doorway, she saw the tears flowing down his cheeks. She knew Elgin was gone.

"Lilli, he was too badly hurt. There was nothing we could do for him," Steve cried grimly.

She can remember Steve's arms around her as she wailed, not

wanting to accept what had just occurred. Through her tears, she struggled to breathe, watching her daughters being escorted into the room. One by one they hugged her and now they, too, were sobbing uncontrollably.

That dark, wet night not only took Elgin's life away, but now it seems as if Lilli's life was gone, too. Now she moved in slow motion as she went through her days and nights. Night time seemed to bring her the most comfort. She retreated to her bed with Gigi and relived all the past years with Elgin. She knew that from the day Elgin entered her life, until that awful night he left her on that dark road, that those would be the very best days of her life. She smiled through her pain and would fall asleep as soon as her Ambien hit its sweet spot.

Every morning, after calls from her daughters and her cousin Phyllis, Lilli would get dressed. Her routine was the same, day in and day out. Feed Gigi, eat some toast, drink some tea and watch the news channel. The hurt still stayed with her daily, never letting up. Little things would remind her of Elgin and her eyes would well up throughout the day.

Lilli made several calls to Linda Richards asking her when this pain would ease up. Linda said she couldn't promise anything in days or months, but through her years of experience she knew it would start to get better and better. She did tell her that she would still experience bad days and nights, but they would get fewer as the time passed.

Lilli told her, "I don't believe you, but what choice do I have but to continue on." Lilli stopped talking.

Linda said, "The pain is raw now, of course you will cry and be angry most of the days, but soon you will smile when you remember Elgin. You will talk about him to your daughters and remember little things that you forgot about him."

Lilli said she had to go and hung up the phone. She walked upstairs to her bedroom, fell into bed and stared at the fan until her eyes closed from the weight of her grief.

Chapter 2

After three months of ignoring phone calls from Elgin's personal assistant, Marie Peters, Lilli made her way down to the building where Elgin worked his way up to senior partner. It was one of the most prestigious law firms between Columbia and Charleston, South Carolina. The name on the building read: Castle, O'Hara, Jackson & Tocci.

Elgin's best friend, Dr. Steve, volunteered to go with Lilli to help clean out Elgin's office. At first, she turned down Steve's offer to help, but then she decided not to put her daughters through this because she really didn't even know if she could handle it. Their daughters had just started rebuilding their lives without their father. This might hamper their progress.

When she pulled into the parking lot and saw Steve's car she knew, with his help, that she could and would do this.

"Hi Steve," Lilli said in a whisper. He came over and hugged her gently. "Thank you for offering to help me with this last piece of Elgin's life."

"He was my best friend since grade school. I miss him each and every day. This is really no inconvenience for me, I wish I could do more for you and the girls. In some strange way I feel like I'm doing this one last thing for Elgin," Steve said as he looked away as if his mind had drifted into the past.

Lilli just nodded and they walked into the building together. They proceeded to the eighth floor and when the doors opened, Lilli just stood there until Steve took her by the elbow and led her down the hall to the office. They entered the huge set of double doors that still bore Elgin's name.

One by one, the procession started again just like it did at the funeral home three months ago. She received lots of sad half smiles, head nods and teary eyes from the many people who were involved in her husband's life on a daily basis. Lisa, one of Elgin's favorite people was the first to approach Lilli.

She spoke softly, "How are you and the girls doing Lilli?"

As both their eyes welled up with tears, Lilli spoke softly, "Oh Lisa, it's so hard without him. I'm so lucky to have our girls, and their wonderful husbands to help me through."

Lisa continued and began to cry, "We all miss him Lilli. There is not a day that goes by that we don't mention Elgin. Everyone agrees that a great piece of the heart of our company is gone now. Elgin would make sure each of us girls had an escort to our car when working late. No one does that now. Things are different without him." Weeping, Lisa stammered back to her desk.

As Lilli made her way down to the huge corner office, others emerged from their offices. Sera, Lauren, Nicole and Larry all surrounded Lilli and once again gave their condolences. She knew that they all attended Elgin's funeral service and burial, but those days of his viewing were now a complete blur to her. Between her Xanax and tears, everything in that short period appeared only in shades of grey and black.

Steve could see that Lilli was becoming more and more upset so he stepped between her and the office staff and guided her into Elgin's office. She was grateful to Steve and appreciated his help. He was such a great friend to Elgin, almost like a brother. He sat beside her at the funeral home and then at the burial proceedings. He held her up as they followed the coffin to the gravesite. Steve had no family of his own so he was always included in all their holidays and family functions. It was so easy and normal that he would help her with her grief now. All the girls agreed that Uncle Steve was a lifesaver during these horrible last three months.

Steve closed Elgin's office door behind them. They both stared at the walls which displayed the plaques of Elgin's life. Lilli absorbed all these pieces and her eyes filled up with tears. Steve moved closer and she put her head on his shoulder. After a few minutes she composed herself and passed her hand over Elgin's huge mahogany desk. "Elgin loved mahogany, did you know his coffin was mahogany?"

Steve looked at her and said, "Lilli, did you forget that I helped you pick it out?"

Lilli smiled, "I guess I did forget, I'm sorry."

"No need to be sorry, those days were rough ones for all of us."

The wooden bookshelves that lined the walls were filled with law books. Those would stay there for the other lawyers. Lilli just wanted Elgin's personal belongings. Lilli sat in his chair and circled the room with her eyes.

She looked over at Steve, "There will be no more cases for Elgin, no files to study, it's really over. His career that he built is gone, just like him."

Steve came over to Lilli and said, "We can get this done together."

She nodded.

Lilli and Steve started to take down the family pictures that Elgin had so proudly displayed. He had been honored by so many organizations for his charity work. She read the plaques out loud to Steve that had come from the Rotary Club, Knights of Columbus, Kiwanis, and Big Brothers and Big Sisters clubs. They both smiled and she put them in one of the boxes that Marie Peters had left for her. She asked Steve to write pictures and plaques on the boxes. She told him she would give them to their girls. He agreed that was a wonderful idea.

Elgin's favorite charity was St Jude. He framed many of the letters they sent him thanking him for his donations and charity drives. She reminded Steve, "Remember when you and Elgin visited St. Jude's Hospital in Memphis? It left such an impression on him. He would talk about it to anyone who would listen. He was taken back by the children who were still smiling while pushing their IV poles around the hospital. Then he told me about how the littlest children were pulled around by their parents in red wagons while their chemo therapy dripped into their little bodies. He couldn't get over their courage and the success rate for the cure. He even ran a Christmas collection at the club last year and raised over ten thousand dollars for them."

Steve smiled, "I remember everything Lilli."

Lilli smiled, "Of course you do, you were right there with him."

She looked down and opened his pending file drawer. It was empty. She raised her eyes and looked over at Steve, "No more files, no more cases. It's really over."

Steve inched closer to Lilli and put his arms on her shoulder, "I miss him too. We will keep him alive with our memories and with the love in our hearts."

Laura, a fellow attorney, entered the office. Laura noticed that Lilli was at Elgin's case pending file drawer and said, "Elgin will never be replaced by me or anyone Lilli. I miss him each day when I come through the doors. He was the only one who had faith in me and insisted I be made partner."

Lilli smiled, "I guess living with four women taught him well about women being equal to men. He loved you Laura. You were like a daughter to him. I'm glad you will be handling his cases. Elgin would be happy about that."

 Just then, there was a soft knock at the door and Henry Castle, the oldest member of the practice walked in. "Am I disturbing you Lilli? I'm heading out to the courthouse but I just had to say, Hi."

Laura hugged Lilli and left the office in tears. Henry came closer to Lilli and kissed her on the cheek. "We are still a family, you can come to us whenever you need something. Remember, when you are up to it, call me and make an appointment to go over the partners insurance policy." Lilli just nodded. Henry left the room and Lilli looked over at Steve. She told him she had forgotten all about the insurance policy. She never thought that she would be the first wife to collect on it, since Henry and Johnny were so much older than Elgin.

Lilli confessed to Steve that she was glad Johnny O'Hara was in court today. "It would be just too hard to talk to Johnny O. Out of all the partners Johnny O and his wife Meg are the ones Elgin and I socialized most with. Please let's get started and pack up the rest of Elgin's things. I just need this to be over with."

Steve nodded, "Tell me what you need next."

Marie entered the office with some smaller boxes for Lilli. "If you need any help, I would be glad…" Lilli cut her off and told her that Steve had offered to help.

Thirty years of Elgin's life was now being boxed up into eight boxes.

Lilli found Elgin's pen collection, still in his top drawer, in the little wooden box he had received from his cousin who was stationed in Russia. She opened the box and started to cry. He had a wonderful collection of pens from Montblanc, David Oscarson and the Visconti labels. Then she picked up his Agatha Christie pen, his favorite. He had read all of the Agatha Christie novels. When he had seen this particular pen, with the snake with the ruby eyes, that was talked about in one of her books, he had to have it. Lilli handed the box to Steve, but put the Agatha Christie pen in her purse. This, she would carry with her from now on.

They finished in silence and when they opened the door to leave,

Elgin's young assistant, Robert Ericcson, ran over to help with the boxes. He was a nice young man from Peru, New York, studying for the bar exam. Lilli told him that Elgin praised him and said he would be a fine young lawyer soon.

"Elgin was always nice to me and answered all my questions even if some of them were obvious. He never made fun of me like Mr. O does," Robert gleamed.

Lilli leaned closer to him, "Johnny doesn't mean it, Robert. Anything he says is not done in a mean-spirited manner. He likes to make people laugh. He makes fun of himself, too."

The goodbyes were all said now. The trunk was packed and Steve turned to Lilli, "Can I buy you lunch before I go to the hospital?"

Her face was full of sadness, "If you don't mind, I'd like to go home and rest now."

She thanked him for all his help. He kissed her cheek and closed her car door. She put down her window and said, "You have been helping me nonstop since the very night Elgin died. I don't think I ever thanked you for all you did for us that awful night."

Steve was the one Lilli called when she was in the ambulance on the way to the hospital with Elgin. Steve helped calm her and the girls when he gave them the news about Elgin. He helped them process this unexpected death of the center of their family. The family was just coming back emotionally from the deaths of their grandparents and Elgin's brother, Lee. How much more were they expected to take?

"No thanks needed, Lilli," said Steve.

On the ride home, Lilli thought back to the two viewing days that had occurred three months earlier. So many people paraded by her chair and extended their condolences. People she never met before who told her how great her husband was to them. She just nodded and then would continue to stare at Elgin in his coffin. At one point, it looked as though he was breathing. When she told her daughter that she could see his chest go up and down, Jeanne called Uncle Steve to talk to her. Steve urged her to leave the funeral home and get some food and liquids in her. She told him there would be plenty of time to leave Elgin alone, she had to stay with him as long as she could now. She marveled at how tall he was. She studied his hands as they lay folded on his chest. How she loved his hands. Those hands lead her through her life for longer than she could remember. She always felt safe when Elgin held her hand through the last few years of loss. Who would have ever thought he was next to leave their family?

When she got the boxes home, Lilli put them in the hall closet. She knew she couldn't deal with emptying them today. Tammy or Noelle could help her with this soon…but not today!

Lilli went up to her bedroom and her loyal pooch followed. She lay next to her in the bed. Elgin knew what to say to her when she was grieving for her parents. He was the one who helped their family come back from their loss. Who would help her now? She was truly all alone for the first time in her life.

Chapter 3

Lilli woke before daybreak and started to think about the early years with Elgin. Thirty-Five years ago, there were only ten thousand people who lived in Summerville. Now, sadly, there were more than two-hundred-fifty thousand, and the town was still growing. Sure, Elgin could have moved them to Charleston, just twenty-three miles away, but it seemed too impersonal and detached to them. Tourists came and went in Charleston. No one ever stayed long enough to know you by name. In Summerville, everyone knew you and your family, including your pets.

Life was just a slower pace in Summerville. You could take Central Avenue right through the center of town where Hutchinson Square awaited you. In Hutchinson Square, you could read all the plaques that lined the sidewalks about the events of the town's history. Lilli recalled sitting on many of the benches there, reading about the past as their own future was unfolding.

A few blocks further down from the Square, you came to the Community Building where you could pick up a brochure and take the walking trail of a homes' tour. Then you would really get a sense of Summerville from days gone by. After church on Sunday, the Jackson Clan would go to Miss Eva's Café. If you were lucky you would run into the professor or once in a while Miss Eva. She was eighty-five years old now, but still sharp as a tack. They would talk about the history of the town. They had lived through all the changes in Summerville and loved to remind you of the past.

Who would have ever imagined that just one month after Christmas, Elgin would be dead? He loved Christmas in Summerville the most, out of any of the rest of the holidays. For many years, Lilli and Elgin would take their girls to the middle of town to watch the parade kick off the holiday season. As little children, they waited anxiously for Santa to arrive on a fire truck and hand out candy canes. Then, that tradition was passed on to their grandkids. The excitement in their eyes was so joyful. This last Christmas, the littlest granddaughters, Stevie and Corbin, took turns on Elgin's shoulders as they waited for Santa. Dane and Daxx thought they were too big for grandpa's shoulders now, so they just popped their heads out in front of their parents as the street started to line up with town folk. Gabby and Nicky ran ahead of the family to try to get the first peek at Santa.   She remembered Elgin saying that it was so wonderful they were all together with their daughters and grandkids. A lot of their friend's children had moved away to Charlotte and Charleston to start their lives. What a treasure to have them all live in Summerville.

She then thought back in detail of that last Christmas morning breakfast at their house with Elgin. The kids came over around eleven after they opened their Santa gifts. The oven put out smells of cinnamon and gingerbread cookies baking. Elgin would put the six of them in a semi-circle in front of the tree. Then he would hand them each a gift. They had to wait for him to count to three before they could rip open the wrapping. He was such a great grandfather. They all waited patiently as he took his sweet time getting to the count of three. There was another tradition…each child, big and small, had to decorate their gingerbread cookie. An extra gift awaited the best decorated cookie each year. Elgin kept the list of last year's winner in his drawer and reminded Lilli whose turn it was to be declared best cookie winner.

All of a sudden, the phone rang and interrupted the rest of Lilli's Christmas memory.

Lilli answered the phone thinking it was one of her daughters, but instead realized it was Anna. Anna had been her friend since their children were in nursery school together. She knew everything about Lilli and Lilli knew everything about Anna and her family.

After an hour of urging her to attend a quiet friends' luncheon at the club next week, Lilli agreed. Anna told her that she had been hiding out in her home for three months and everyone missed her.

"I gave strict instructions to everyone not to question you or ask how you are doing," she said.

Lilli told her that her hair was a mess. She had roots about a half inch long. She wasn't expecting to see anyone. She didn't feel the need to get her hair dyed. She finally gave in and told Anna when she went to the grocery store that she would get a box of hair dye and do it herself over the weekend.

Anna told her to just go over to Kristin's hair salon and get it done by her. "She always does it so pretty for you."

Lilli told her, "I just couldn't face all the women in the salon yet. I love Kristin but there are just too many gossips in her shop. I don't want everyone talking to me about Elgin."

Anna relented, "OK, dye your own hair the best you can."

They made a date for next Tuesday. Lilli picked Tuesday because it was the slowest day in the club. Not many people were at Summerville Manor Oaks Club on a cold Tuesday before spring.

The day had finally arrived and Anna would be picking Lilli up in less than hour. She was rushing around putting concealer on to try to hide the dark circles under her eyes. She dabbed a small amount of taupe eye shadow on her eyelids and put some pale pink lipstick on. Her hair lay flat on her head pulled back by her signature leather headband. It wasn't her usual look but at least the white hair had been erased.

She looked at herself one more time in her bathroom mirror, "It's the best I can do. Who cares anyway?"

Anna picked Lilli up at noon and they set off to the club.

Lilli seemed nervous and looked at Anna, "I don't know how I can go into the club without Elgin. I don't know how to live without him."

Anna assured her once again, "Your friends will help you get through this horrible time in your life. Elgin would not want you to live the rest of your life locked up in your bedroom. You would be doing him a great disservice by sitting there, day in and day out grieving. You would destroy all the happy memories of the days and nights you spent there together."

Lilli managed a half smile, "They were the best years ever."

She sat quietly for the rest of the ride.

Upon arrival at the club, Lilli was greeted warmly by the valet, Marc. Francine, the hostess, came around from the desk and extended her condolences. "We all loved Mr. Jackson and will miss him dearly."

Lilli nodded and smiled and walked behind Anna to their table.

Lilli looked around the dining room and thought how everything looked the same. Why was everything the same and she was so different? Nothing had changed except her life.

In the years since the children were all grown and leading their own lives, the club had become Lilli's life. Elgin spent many afternoons doing business on the golf course. He planned many fundraisers for his various charities. Lilli helped chair the annual Christmas Toys for Tots fundraiser. Her three girls had their weddings at the club.

Friends joked that Elgin and Lilli owned stock in the club. As soon as she was seated at the table and had her first glass of wine in months, that old familiarity started to take over. She suddenly felt strangely comfortable once again.

Conversations started with Irene and Rosie and went on for three hours. It was as if this time together had brought her back to her former days at the club when Elgin was still alive. Lilli apologized to her friend Irene for not answering her phone calls. "I just wasn't ready to talk to you." Irene nodded and said she understood perfectly.

Irene and Lilli spent many mornings antiquing and crafting. Irene taught Lilli how to knit and make floral arrangements for her home. Irene even talked Elgin and Lilli, along with her husband Jack, into square dancing lessons. That only lasted one short winter. Their husbands always seemed to break down the square and just couldn't get into it like a real square dancer might. They had many laughs over those days as part of the Bridgeville Rocks Square Dancing Club.

The time spent with her friends was a comfort and ended all too quickly. Lilli couldn't believe it was after three o'clock already. She said she had to get home to take Gigi out for a walk. Her mind had moved on to the dog, her new found constant.

Lilli waited as Marc brought Anna's car around the circle. She hugged her friends warmly and told them she had a good time and would meet them again next Tuesday, if possible. Everyone smiled and agreed it was a date.

The next month found Lilli leaving her house every Tuesday at noon, but then she would be back up in her bedroom by six with her dinner tray. Her friends suggested that they all meet for dinner with their husbands. These men were all very good friends of Elgin, but Lilli flatly refused.

She just wasn't ready to bring herself back to the place where Elgin had sat beside her for more years than she could remember. Also, no one knew but Lilli had to be tucked into the safe haven of her bedroom before dark. No one realized that she was still afraid to get into her car after dark since that wet, starless night on Hilltop Road. This was her secret now. She hoped her daughters wouldn't figure it out. Not yet.

The silver XJR jaguar that Lilli bought Elgin for his last birthday sat covered up in their garage since the night of the accident when her son-in-law Carlton picked it up from Hilltop Road and parked it in the garage. He made sure he covered it up so Lilli didn't have to look at it. Each time she looks at the silhouette of the car hidden under the beige cover she thinks how strange it is that the car didn't have a scratch on it and yet Elgin was dead. The car, too, now seemed dead to her.

Chapter 4

Lunches continued throughout the summer and Lilli had now re-connected with most of the Club members. At first, many of the ladies dared not speak about Elgin in fear of upsetting Lilli, but everyone soon started to talk about Elgin and all the good times they shared. This made Lilli smile. Lilli was introduced to the new tennis coach and golf pro. Some of her friends were going to try their hand at tennis in the fall and others were continuing to take their yearly golf lessons.

The tennis coach, Luke Alexander, invited Lilli to join her friends in his ladies' foursome tennis group. Lilli kindly refused. "Maybe next spring," she said. He assured her he would remind her. They both smiled, and he left.

The fall found Lilli getting into a familiar routine of the club's women's outings, and meetings for preparations for the Christmas Club toy drive. She was keeping herself quite busy now and it felt good not to be sad every minute of every day. She still had her moments when she would regress back into the darkest time of her life, but like Linda Richards said, it would get easier.

Christmas came and went with some traditions kept, but, for the most part, it was on the quiet side for everyone's sake. Elgin's chair at the table was left empty, as she had placed a Christmas teddy bear made out of Elgin's red flannel shirt on it, so no one would sit there.

They still took the children to the parade and they all went to Lilli's house for the cookie decorating contest, but it was so different now. Even the littlest kids could feel it. They asked if grandpa was having Christmas in heaven with the angels. They asked if he could come back for Christmas. Tears welled up in everyone's eyes as they tried to make sense of it for the kids. It didn't make sense to explain it to these little children. Unnecessary, unexpected, death can never be explained away.

Passing out the presents was now handed down to Lilli, and once the count was over, most of the emphasis from the kids was on the toys. No more questions from the kids. Then came cookie decorating and eating dinner. Everyone was gone by seven.

Lilli made her way upstairs with Gigi and lay in bed and reread all the cards the children had made for her. How innocent were their words. They were untouched by the unkind world that surrounds us all. Lilli thought about how the next month would bring all the memories of the last year of her life. In less than a month, it would be one year since Elgin was KILLED on Hilltop Road. There were still no suspects and it seemed as if the police had forgotten all about Elgin's homicide by vehicle.

Lilli went to the office of Linda Richards as January 20th neared. Linda assured her this would be the hardest day, but she would and should do something to get her family through it.

Linda tried to encourage her, "Show your strength to the children, big and small. Don't try to brush it aside as just a normal day or bury it under the rug as to hide it. Everyone knows the day and is expecting it to be hard."

Lilli said she would gather the family for a dinner at her house.

Linda said, "That's a terrific idea. A light has gone out in your family and it is up to you to lead them back from the darkness."

Lilli sighed, "I am so lost myself…how do I lead them?"

"You are their mom and with that comes the instinct to protect. It is there even if you can't feel it right now. The love you have for your family and the love you still feel for Elgin will show you how to do it. Trust yourself."

Linda asked about the nightmares and Lilli did confess that they were getting less. Linda smiled, "I'm so happy to hear that." They both smiled. Lilli left and drove straight home.

Once home, she made lists of foods to prepare for the family gathering. She would have all of Elgin's favorite dishes. She set up the dining room, as it was set so many nights for family dinners.

She then made her calls one by one. First, she told Jeanne to make sure she brought the children to this dinner. She wanted them to also celebrate grandpa's life.

Jeanne admitted, "I hate it when people use the term 'celebrate their life'. Dad is dead. He's never coming back. The kids will feel like we are celebrating his birthday." Lilli assured her once they were all together it would be ok.

Lilli made calls to Noelle and Tammy and everyone was on board for the third Saturday in January. Lilli had two weeks to try to get herself to do this. She knew she had to.

Chapter 5

The anniversary of Elgin's death was upon the family. They all congregated in the Jackson's living room and the grief was as raw and painful as the night of the accident. Trying to sound almost cheerful, Lilli spoke first, "Tonight, I have set the dining room table and we will all take our places as we did in the past but this time, we will leave Dad's seat empty. We will toast him and eat his favorite dinner."

Noelle responded, "I can't eat when I'm upset."

Lilli told her, "Get the Cake-bread wine out of the wine cabinet and have Carlton open it. I'm sure that after a few glasses of wine, you will eat something."

Noelle put her head down as tears welled up in her big brown eyes. Her long black hair covered her face as a shroud as she wept.

Gabby and Nicky, the oldest grandchildren, led Corbin, Stevie, Dane and Daxx into the playroom. Gabby made a card for Elgin. Nicky signed it first and helped the little ones do the same. They put it in an envelope and sealed it with lots of 'X's' and 'O's' on it. With Tammy's supervision, they attached the card to a bunch of helium balloons as they would soon send it off to heaven for Elgin.

Gabby said, "We are sending balloons to heaven just like the little girl in the story I read."

Everyone was standing on the front lawn for the launch of the balloons and you could see the tears falling through their smiles. Tammy spoke first, breaking the silence.

Through her sobs, she said, "We love you, Dad."

Lilli choked and said, "It's time to toast Dad, let's go inside."

The dining room was not set up to par the way Lilli had done in the past, but it was still elegant. Lilli started, "This was Dad's favorite wine and I'd like you all to have a drink in his honor." Everyone raised their glasses and Lilli continued to lead her children. "Elgin, we all love and miss you and you will always live on in our minds and especially in our hearts."

The girls continued to wipe away tears, but to Lilli's amazement she didn't shed any at that table. She had to be their rock now and so she went around the table and hugged each of them and in that small gesture they all knew it was time for the healing to really start.

Chapter 6

After a year of delightful lunches, and some return to normalcy for Lilli, Savannah Grace suggested, "Lilli, let's get back into golf or, maybe we could take some tennis lessons from the new tennis pro. We could get on a doubles team and get some much-needed exercise."

Lilli dismissed the idea without a second thought, but Savannah Grace kept at her until she finally agreed. Although Lilli dragged her feet about signing up for the series of twelve beginner lessons, but finally did. When the day of the first lesson rolled around, it happened to be a dreary, but warm spring day in April. The last thing Lilli wanted to do today was play tennis. The sky was darkening, and Lilli hoped that by the time she arrived at the club, the heavens would open drowning the tennis court. Unfortunately, that didn't happen and before she knew it, Savannah Grace was introducing her once again to Luke Howard, the tennis pro.

Savannah Grace and Carol Ann were right. He was tall, tan, and had all around good looks. Luke Howard had come to the south from Pittsburgh, Pennsylvania. His father was a self-made multimillionaire, who was in the steel business. Luke had no interest in the business world, in general. He had no interest in any sort of politics or religion, and he had no interest in a serious relationship. He was just floundering out there not knowing who he was or where he belonged. Could he really be happy teaching middle aged men and women to swing a tennis racquet?

Luke had graduated from Harvard, with honors. Studies had always come easy to Luke. He had many casual friends, but he never quite cemented any relationships or hung with anyone. Years ago, some of his Harvard buddies asked him to go to Europe with them for summer break, but he had never been interested in going to other countries. He wanted to travel the United States, to each state…all fifty of them. He did a fine job, too, in crisscrossing the United States. He was into the party hardy scene. So far, he had traveled and spent time in about thirty of the fifty states. Unfortunately for him, he didn't remember much about his travels except for the many hangovers he endured the day after.

His father's money allowed him to travel and enjoy the sweet things that life could offer, although, his easy ride came to an abrupt end one day last year. His father, John Alexander Howard, whose health was now failing, asked Luke to come home to Pittsburgh and help him manage his company. It was an ultimatum for Luke to settle down and grow up. Luke flatly refused. His monthly stipend ended at the age of forty-six. What would he do now? Where would he go?

He took the maps from his car trunk and thought about all the places he had visited during his travels around the United States. He felt strangely drawn back to the small southern town of Summerville, South Carolina. He didn't exactly know when he visited Summerville because that was the year that vodka had been his best friend. He stayed only a few days and most of his memories were still a blur. He did remember that he visited in the winter, maybe December or January. The way he remembered Summerville was that it wasn't cold, and the flowers were still in bloom. He liked the idea of warm winters, but hated Florida. He wasn't crazy about the west side of the United States. He would get out of Pittsburgh, as it was too damn cold and dreary. He needed that Carolina blue sky and warm sunshine. Yes, he would go back to Summerville and try to make sense of his life. He aimed his car south and before he knew it, he was pulling into a motel in the small hamlet of Summerville. He would get a good night's sleep and then start the next stage of his life in the morning.

The next morning, he drove around the town looking for a place to live and found a very nice condominium complex right in the heart of town, called the Summerville Commons Townhouses. He immediately found the landlord, Frankie B., and he went into his office and signed a month to month lease just in case things didn't work out for him in this sleepy hide-a-way town. This is where he would settle down for the time being and see what Summerville would bring to him. He wasn't very good at much, so when he opened up a copy of the Summerville Daily Recorder Newspaper, the only thing that fit him was the small two-line ad seeking a tennis pro at the very affluent Manor Oaks Country Club. At the age of forty-seven, he would have to fend for himself for the first time. He was strangely excited about this new concept. He knew he would have to make some changes, quickly. No more tequila or vodka, at least not for a while. He had to get on track now. He had no one watching his back. He was all alone.

In his forty-seven years, Luke took more tennis lessons than he could remember. Reflecting, he remembered taking tennis and golf lessons around the age of seven. He had also played on the semi-pro tennis team during his stint at boarding school and in college, too. It occurred to him now, that he might have just found his niche in life in the Summerville Daily Recorder Newspaper. He also rationalized that it wouldn't be too hard to teach some middle-aged men and women how to keep the ball inbounds while playing doubles.

Luke had an easygoing way about him and could charm the ladies with his intoxicating smile. He exhibited this by sweet talking his way into the tennis pro's job at the club the very next day. The club's manager, Julie, who was usually a tough nut to crack, fell under his spell and hired him on the spot. Way in the back of her mind, Julie thought to herself that Luke was the best-looking thing to come to Summerville in a decade. She was happy to be the one to keep him around and even secretly thought she might be the one to snag him sometime down the road. His yearly salary was now half the yearly allowance he was receiving from his father but he didn't seem to mind.

Chapter 7

His first six months went along very well. His charisma gained the confidence of the club members easily. While he did seem genuine about enjoying their company, the male members of the club had their doubts about his intentions towards the aging women members. Most of the women thought their husbands were jealous of his good looks and hard body. In truth, he did seem more interested in flirting with the widows and divorcees than the married members. Still, no rumors surfaced about any improprieties concerning him. Luke harbored a few secrets though, and this small sleepy town would soon be privy to them. Everyone has secrets buried deep inside them, but his were so far down, maybe they would never resurface. Maybe with the right person, and this new life, someday he could release them and finally be saved.

After Savannah reintroduced Luke to Lilli, the lesson progressed very slowly. First, Luke taught Lilli how to hold her racquet, then where to stand when serving, and finally how to lob the ball over the net. Lilli did have very good hand-eye coordination and the series of lessons might even prove to make her a worthy opponent on the ladies' doubles team. Luke and Lilli made another date for her next lesson.

"I'm so glad to have made your acquaintance Mrs. Jackson," said Luke. "I can't believe you never played tennis, you are a natural."

Lilli replied suspiciously, "I bet you say that to all the old ladies you teach."

Luke raised an eyebrow and said, "I didn't say it to any of your friends, did I?" He smiled, "I don't think of you as an old lady."

"Well, I am," said Lilli, turning her head, smiling suspiciously and excitedly at the same time and walked away.

Lunch followed with Amanda, the youngest of the over forties group. They giggled at how silly they felt taking tennis lessons at their age. They all commented on the good looks and great body of the new tennis pro. After lunch, Lilli headed for the parking lot. The rain started to pound the club-house and everyone seemed to be waiting in line for the valet parkers. Lilli didn't want to wait so she asked for her keys and ran towards her car with her purse over her head. She was startled as an umbrella suddenly shielded her from the rain.

"Hi Mrs. Jackson," said Luke. "Just thought an old lady like your-self could use a little help getting into your car."

Lilli said, "Yes, I could, thank you so much. I guess it's true that boy scouts like you are trained to help old ladies cross the street."

Luke chuckled as Lilli giggled. He opened her car door and she jumped in getting some much-needed relief from the rain that had already drenched her.

Her hair laid dripping on her shoulders as Luke leaned into her car and said, "I look forward to our next meeting."

"Me, too," Lilli smiled and turned the key to the ignition…of the car.

Chapter 8

Lilli went home before dark as she had routinely done for months, but this time it was different. She didn't bring a tray to her bedroom. With her faithful dog Gigi at her side, Lilli ate in the family room. For the first time, she didn't drift back to that awful night when she lost Elgin forever. Gigi cuddled on the couch close to Lilli's leg. Lilli stayed there for a while and as she stroked Gigi's soft white furry body, she thought about her day. She thought about how she surprised herself as she returned one tennis ball after another over the net effortlessly. She thought about the rain and she thought about Luke Howard. She thought about Luke more than she wanted to and she felt guilty because she had had fun. She felt shame because no man had ever appealed to her, even a little, since she met Elgin. She thought to herself that she was just a lonely, old, foolish widow. Then, as to instill it deep into her brain she said out loud, "You're an old fool Lilli Belle Jackson." She turned the television on and watched the news for the next few hours.

It was time for bed, and with Gigi trailing behind, Lilli carried her tray into the kitchen and put her dishes into the dishwasher. She then turned out the lights and proceeded, with her pooch in hand, to the bedroom. Gigi was once Elgin's dog, following him around from room to room, and sleeping on his side of the bed. Now Lilli and Gigi were inseparable. Even Gigi knew that Elgin wasn't coming back, and Lilli was the only one there for her. She took off her makeup and surveyed her wrinkles in the mirror. She put cream on her face, something she hadn't done in months. She creamed the dry, spotted skin on her arms and then on her legs. She realized that she was starting to care about herself again. She closed her eyes and imagined Elgin was telling her how good she smelled and how soft she felt. He never forgot to compliment her. She missed that attention and that's what she attributed her thoughts of Luke to…just a normal craving for some attention.

The next morning came and went very quickly with Lilli doing odds and ends around the house. Things she hadn't done since Elgin died. Things that seemed so superficial to her, have all at once became important again. She went through the stack of mail on her desk that her daughter, Noelle, had divided into piles. Noelle named them the important papers, and then there was the unimportant pile. Her monthly bills had been taken care of, but the unimportant remained unopened. There were subscriptions that had to be renewed and charities that were asking for donations, which had to be answered, if only with a check. One by one, Lilli got through the unimportant pile in about two hours. She sifted through tons of mail order catalogues and she kept only the ones she regularly ordered from, mostly the children clothing magazines. She worked nonstop and filled up the large trash can in her kitchen. She finally got through all the junk mail and came upon a college for seniors' brochure. She thumbed through the brochure and highlighted a few things that looked interesting to her. She thought to call her cousin Phyllis and maybe they would take a course next semester. She then thought about the classes she had taken, especially the Feng Shui which she loved. Today, through cleaning out her surplus of mail, she started to create a much-needed balance in her life. She knew that harmony would soon follow if her teachings came to pass. She had learned that she must organize and keep things in some sort of order to find good fortune, health, and good energy in life. Lilli knew that she was lacking those things.

"Feng Shui taught me to clean up all the clutter and messes around me. Then I will find good chi, we'll see," she said out loud.

She thought back about how Elgin laughed, as she placed a dozen or so green plants around the house so that their lives would be enhanced with good chi. She took care of the plants diligently because if they didn't stay vibrant and healthy her chi was sure to turn bad. It was about this time in their lives that Elgin brought home the tiniest Maltese puppy that one of his grateful clients gave him. This puppy came into their lives over Lilli's objections. Elgin reminded her that Feng Shui teaches you that pets, along with plants, are supposed to bring out good chi and a loving spirit in everyone, and she really wasn't going to go against the teachings of ancient wise men. A smile came over her and she said out loud "Elgin, you were right as usual, your Gigi has brought out my loving spirit."

After lunch, Lilli went into the sunroom and started looking through her catalogues when the front doorbell rang. There stood her oldest daughter, Jeanne, with her two beautiful children, Gabby and Nicky. They had come to check up on her and ask her to dinner.

It was hard to decline the dinner offer with Gabby begging like she did, "Please Gram, come over to our house, Mommy is going to make your favorite dinner."

Lilli knew she wasn't up to that hurdle just yet. Lilli explained that she was tired from all the little things she had straightened out in her house that day. Of course, she didn't share her fear of the night. Besides, that seemed to be her time to spend with Elgin. When nighttime fell, so did she. She fell back into the past and thumbed through old photos and newspaper clippings. She saw all the wonderful things Elgin did in the community and through the clubs he belonged to. She especially loved to read all the letters she had collected from Elgin over the past thirty-five years. Then it would happen all over again as the night time reminded her of the accident. The darkness brought on a very private grief. She couldn't share the night with anyone but Elgin yet… she fell asleep with Gigi cuddled up on one side of her and a few photo albums of her life with Elgin on the other side.

Lilli awoke about 3 a.m. realizing that she had fallen asleep in her clothes again. She got into her P.J.'s and cleared her bed of all the albums. She got under her down comforter and fell back asleep with thoughts of Elgin once more. She was hoping she would dream about him, but she never did. She wanted him to talk to her in her deepest dreams, but he would never come to her. She wanted to know if he was with his brother Lee who had died of cancer just a year before Elgin. Elgin adored Lee and missed him every day of that year he lived without him. No one would have ever imagined that Elgin would be sharing eternity with Lee so soon. She wondered if he missed her and the girls? Was heaven as wonderful as they had been led to believe in Bible study as well as by their church? By the time 8 a.m. rolled around, she was wide-awake. It was time to get her day started.

Chapter 9

Once she started to focus on the day, she realized she really had nothing to do. She had no one to see and no one to take care of anymore except for her dog. She thought to herself that she was this lonely, old, sad character in life's new play. Could she ever get back from this part she was now forced to act? First, she had to figure out where she was. She knew she could never have a life with Elgin again. She knew that her role as a mother had diminished over the past years as her daughters became mothers themselves.

It seemed unfair that in the prime of her life she would be left out there alone to start over again, and to figure things out for herself. She was so secure in her life with Elgin, it was just so natural, exactly where she truly belonged. It was her place in the grand scheme of this thing we call our destiny. Her home was where her story began and now it seemed to have ended there.

She had enjoyed the country club life with all its trimmings. Since Elgin secured his position as partner, they didn't have any more money worries. She could have gone anyplace she wanted and bought anything. Funny how insignificant it seems that what they were working toward for the last thirty-five years doesn't matter worth a damn now. She would give all that up for one more night with her husband.

She then thought back on all the nights they made love. Elgin was such a gentleman in every way. Even when they made love, he made sure she was enjoying it as much as he did. He always made her feel special and she longed for his hands to caress her body once again. If only she could feel his soft lips press against hers.

Saturday nights always seemed to be their night for making love. After a few drinks at the club and some romantic dancing, it was the perfect way to end their hectic week. Elgin said he agreed with the song about dancing and how it felt like making love. When they got home, usually about midnight, they would relax and enjoy each other as husband and wife and fall asleep in each other's arms. The regularity of the Saturday night act and the gentleness he gave to her always made her feel special. Lilli thought back to how Elgin used to put his leg over hers or touched her hand as they slept each night. He always told her that he had to touch some part of her when he slept. He claimed it was the only way he could fall asleep. How she missed his touch. Since Elgin's death, Saturday night had become the night that Lilli hated the most…the loneliest night of the week.

Chapter 10

The tennis lessons continued, and, to Lilli's surprise, she started to look forward to the hour with Luke and her friends. Rosie and Irene would quiz Luke about his life, but Lilli realized that with all their questioning they didn't seem to get much from him. They did learn that his family was prominent in Pittsburgh. He was an only child, and his mother had died when he was only ten years old. His father shipped him off to military school after he married his secretary, only three months after his mother was buried.

Luke said, "My stepmom, Arlene, seemed nice but I really didn't see much of her since she sent me away to school." Luke seemed a little hurt by how quickly his father remarried, but still it was not easy to read him. He offered no other personal information but was polite and straight to the point with the questions asked of him by the women. He seemed like a man who had well insulated himself from hurt, or for that matter, any other feelings. Lilli knew he was quiet, complicated, mysterious, and it puzzled her as to why she still found him very engaging. How could a person who seemed so aloof still be so interesting to her? Elgin always said what was on his mind and when he became quiet, Lilli could open him up in a heartbeat.

Luke got Lilli and her friends into an over 40's women's tennis group. The group met every Friday at noon and played for an hour or so. After tennis, everyone would shower, then eat lunch.

After leaving Manor Oaks, it was the same routine for Lilli. Go to the grocery store, cleaners, bank, and then home to her puppy and her haven before dark. It wasn't for lack of invitations that Lilli stayed home on the weekends, but she still wasn't ready to step out after dark. She wondered if this obsession with the night would ever leave her. Maybe she should talk to someone? Should she confide in Phyllis or one of her daughters? Maybe she should go back to Linda, her grief counselor. She knew she couldn't continue with this unreasonable fear of the night and darkness.

Suddenly, it was winter again and that meant that Lilli and her family were closing in on the second anniversary of Elgin's death, but first, her family would have to face their second Christmas without Elgin. This year had to be different, Lilli would insist that Jeanne have her traditional brunch, and everyone meet there to celebrate with the children. Last year everyone congregated at Lilli's house and sat around and pretended not to be sad for the sake of the children. Then one by one the girls would disappear into another room while they cried over the loss of their father. Yes, this year had to be different. As of late, she hadn't thought about that horrible dark night as frequently as she had in the past. She told herself this didn't mean that she was forgetting Elgin, but only that she was getting accustomed to living with her good memories of him. In some way, these memories were quite comforting to her and lessened the heartache. It was time to bar the door from the anger she felt. She had to stop being mad at God and the driver because nothing would bring Elgin back to her.

She started to remember the early years. She had fond memories of when they took trips with their children to Hilton Head, Myrtle

Beach, and Florida. Thoughts of these times made her smile.

Linda was right, finally she had started to remember the good times she had shared with Elgin and her daughters.

Chapter 11

It was late one cold Saturday afternoon in March when she returned home from her usual chores. She came in the house expecting Gigi, but there was no Gigi. She combed the house and finally found the little Maltese curled up in the corner of her bedroom. She bent down next to her little companion to see what was wrong. She picked her up and realized she was quite limp. Lilli panicked and called the vet. The vet told her to bring her right in before they closed for the weekend.

Lilli raced to the vet's office repeating to Gigi, "You have to get well, you can't die, I can't lose you, too."

As she parked her car, a familiar voice shouted hello from across the parking lot. She shot a quick look toward the back of her car and saw Luke standing there with a very tiny kitten. She told him, "Something is wrong with my dog and I have to get in to see the doctor before they close."

He told her, "I hope everything works out for you."

Lilli was gone before he reached his car.

Lilli's visit lasted about two hours before her dog and the vet emerged not knowing much more than when she first got there. Dr. Vanessa Matthews gave Lilli a lot of educated guesses but no conclusive answers for her sick little dog. The vet's words echoed in her mind as she drove home, "When the blood results come in, we will decide what treatment path to take. For now, just take Gigi home and make her as comfortable as possible. No restrictions of food or activity, I will call you Monday."

Lilli went home and tried to feed Gigi, but the poor little thing just moaned with pain. She just lay there on the bed with Lilli and together they fell asleep.

Gigi would periodically moan, and Lilli would stroke her, assuring her she would not let her die—then she remembered that this was the same empty promise she made Elgin. Lilli cried herself to sleep. She slept uneasily until the phone rang, quickly composing herself to answer it.

To her surprise it was Luke calling. He apologized and said, "I know I'm not allowed to call a club member, but I had to see if you and your dog were okay. You looked so scared at the vet's office this afternoon."

Lilli was so glad to have someone to confide in that she started to tell him about the vet visit and her fears of losing this little creature that she had grown so accustomed to over the past two years. He tried to comfort her and assure her that the vet was very knowledgeable and would find out how to cure her dog.

He asked, "When is your next visit?"

Lilli told him she had to wait until Monday for the first blood results and then would return on Wednesday for the result of all the tests.

Lilli then asked, "Why were you at the vet?"

Luke told her, "I was visiting the vet with my new kitten Snickers."

He had just taken one of the kittens from his landlord, Frankie B.

He said, "Although Frankie B is usually a very quiet man, he talked a blue streak until I relented and adopted the runt of the litter. This is the first time I've ever owned a pet. Snickers is the first living thing I've had to take care of beside myself. I've never even owned a gold fish."

Then he told her that he did swallow some goldfish soaked in beer one time at a frat party. Luke continued, "I can't believe that I am reading books about kittens and I just hope that I am doing everything right."

Lilli spoke effortlessly, "Gigi wasn't really my responsibility until Elgin died, but now she is more than a responsibility, she is my constant friend, my main companion who helps fill up my lonely dark nights."

Luke suddenly felt an overwhelming sense of compassion for her, something he wasn't quite sure about how to handle. He told her, "I hope I feel that way about Snickers in time." He said he was doubtful, but she assured him that the kitten would grow on him and soon be a great companion. "I plan on giving it the old college try." His voice saddened, "I've always been sort of a loner, most of the time by choice, and now this little thing is always scampering around my feet looking for my attention."

Lilli assured him that everything would work out for the best, just hang in for a few months. After twenty minutes of an unexpected heart to heart conversation, Lilli thanked him for calling and said goodbye. She thought it was nice of him to call but she wouldn't tell anyone from the club. She knew she could confide in her cousin Phyllis, though. He would certainly get in trouble or even worse, some nosey old biddies might get the wrong idea about her and the handsome tennis pro.

The next few days Lilli stuck close to home and tried to will her puppy to get better. Finally, Wednesday rolled around with the dark clouds and a rain that never stopped falling. As Lilli pulled up to the vet's office, she noticed Luke sitting in his car. She asked him, "Is your kitten okay?"

"Oh yes," he replied, "I got rained out at the club, so I decided to check up on you and Gigi."

Lilli was very surprised and more than a little flattered. Once again, he came over to protect her from the rain with his umbrella. This time he covered up her sick little puppy, too.

Dr. Alison Lucas stuck her head out of the examining room, "I'll be with Gigi in a few minutes Mrs. Jackson."

Luke said he never saw that vet and Lilli told Luke that Dr. Lucas was just as good as Dr. Mathews. As she waited for the vet, Luke continued to give her encouragement. "Lilli, I know from doctors in general that if something was drastically wrong, they would have called you already."

Lilli replied, "You're probably right, but I can't lose my dog, she just has to get better."

After Dr. Lucas read the blood results, she told Lilli that Gigi had Lyme disease. It was serious, but she said that Gigi would get better. It would take her a good month to get her back to her old self again with the help of an antibiotic twice a day and a pain pill to relieve the joint pain. Lilli was relieved but was still baffled as to how her dog got this disease. Lilli caressed Gigi as the vet spoke to her. Luke watched Lilli intently and marveled at how gentle and loving she was. He noticed how naturally pretty Lilli was, too. She wore only a little lipstick and her skin was so silky smooth. He was guessing she was around forty-four or forty-five years old. He thought she had to be the youngest one in the over 40's tennis group. All the other women had weathered faces and frail looking bodies with toothpick legs. She did have a few wrinkles around her eyes, but so did he. Her body was athletic looking and muscular. When Lilli smiled, her face lit up and it made him smile, too. For some reason, this woman had touched him. Maybe it was because she had lost her husband in a tragedy way too soon in her life as he did, suffering the loss of his mother. He felt linked to her in some uncanny, unexplainable way.

Luke always felt like he was running away but didn't know from what. Maybe it was from the sadness of losing his mother who he adored or maybe he was running away from his father who so easily replaced his mother. His father wanted to make a clone of himself out of Luke. Luke knew this and decided to be the direct opposite. All his life he was self-destructing by drinking and wandering around aimlessly. Whatever the case was then, now he was glad to be settled in Lilli's company. He wanted to spend more time with her but how could he manage that? She was a rich widow and he was a lowly tennis pro with no past worth talking about, no family ties, and now no money. She would only think he wanted to fleece her out of hers. He tried to open up to her on more than one occasion, but he would always shut down after a few minutes as he caught himself going further into his life.

After Lilli paid the huge vet bill, Luke walked her back to the car. Lilli gently placed her pooch on the seat then thanked Luke for coming to her rescue with his umbrella again. He said he was glad that Gigi's prognosis was good, and he hoped to see her at the club soon. Then he turned and walked to his car. She couldn't help herself but watched him as he folded down the umbrella and got in. She wanted to call out to him but didn't know what else to say since she already thanked him. She knew they couldn't go to the diner for a cup of coffee because she had her dog with her and she certainly couldn't let her nosey next-door neighbors, Jenn and William, see him come into her house.

Like Elgin always said, "When you have neighbors like Jenn and William, you really don't need an alarm system in your home."

They knew everyone's comings and goings and told anyone who cared to listen about it. She would never be able to explain Luke to them. They would never believe her.

Chapter 12

It was spring again and the air was warm once more. The over forty ladies' doubles tennis group was ready to start up again. Lilli was excited to get back to the club and see her friends and play tennis. Her dog was on the mend, so she was able to go to the club with a clear head today. She showered, blew her hair, and put on lipstick and under eye concealer. She was trying to hide the crow's feet that had popped up in the last year which made her feel very old. She put on a new tennis outfit that she bought a few months ago and off she went.

There was something different about today, she had a spring in her step. She convinced herself she was feeling good that her dog was better, and it wasn't because she was going to see Luke in an hour. As she arrived just inside the front door of the clubhouse, she literally ran into Luke. He apologized for bumping into her and told her that he was running late for a lesson. He was kind enough to ask about Gigi, with a great big ear-to-ear smile Lilli said, "She is doing wonderful, thank you for asking."

He smiled back at her and said, "Great, I'll see you in an hour on the court," and off he went.

Why did seeing this man make her smile? They barely knew each other. He meant nothing to her—he was just her tennis teacher. Besides all of that, he was so much younger than her. They had nothing at all in common. Was that the attraction? Once again, she told herself to stop being an old fool and act her age. She was embarrassed at the thoughts she was having about Luke. They weren't sexual in any way, but they made her feel alive again and she had to remain true to Elgin. She couldn't disrespect her marriage or life with Elgin for anyone. EVER!

One by one her ladies group poured into the locker room. Everyone put on their tennis shoes and got their racquets. Gina was the first to notice Lilli's glow. Then Lisa and Kira noticed it, too. Lilli said it was because her dog was on the mend and she was finally feeling that the cards weren't stacked up against her.

It was funny how Tina popped out of nowhere and said in her sweet southern way, "Lilli Belle Jackson, I'd say you had the glow of a woman in love or at least in lust."

Lilli just laughed along with the other ladies. Everyone continued to get ready and proceeded to the tennis court for their match.

Luke came over to Lilli and apologized for giving her the bum's rush before but said he was really thrilled that Gigi was doing better.

"By the way," he said, "Snickers is really growing on me just like you said she would."

Lilli noticed that the whole group had their eyes glued to her and Luke and she then cut it short by saying, "Great."

Then out of nowhere, Luke whispered to Lilli, "Will you join me for a cup of coffee some night to discuss our animals?"

Lilli could feel her cheeks turning red and she answered in a faint voice, "Yes!" before she even realized what she had done.

He said, "I'll call you soon." He then went over to the other side of the court.

Once they got back into the locker room, her group surrounded her all eager to find out what he said to her.

She assured them, "He only wanted to know how my dog was doing because he ran into me at the vet's office when Gigi was so sick."

She just couldn't tell them what a fool she'd just been in accepting his invitation for a cup of coffee. That had to remain a secret.

Chapter 13

Six days went by and still no call from Luke, so she just figured he had thought better of it. Then to Lilli's surprise, Luke wasn't at the club when she met with the tennis group the following day. She didn't want to bring any attention to herself by mentioning his absence, so she just let it slide by until lunch. On her way to the dining room she heard two of her favorite waitresses, Amanda and Anne Marie talking about Luke.

She casually mentioned to them, "Luke missed his tennis club's tournament today. Is everything all right with him?"

They told her that his stepmother called the club and he immediately flew back to Pittsburgh because his father had a major stroke. In some small way, it made Lilli feel better to know Luke didn't blow her off because he realized he made a mistake in saying that he would call. She didn't feel like such a complete fool now, just half of a fool.

The next Sunday, after returning from church, there was a message from Luke on her answering machine.

He said "Hi Lilli, its Luke. I'm so sorry I didn't call sooner, but I had to fly back to Pittsburgh. My father had a stroke, but he has stabilized for now. I was wondering if we could get together for dinner. That is, if you haven't already made plans. Please call me back."

Lilli was a little shaken with excitement about the call, so she sat down to analyze the situation. If she called, she would hope Luke wouldn't get the wrong idea and think she was a desperate old lady dying for companionship or even something more. If she didn't call, he might get the wrong idea and think she thought he was beneath her. She would just have to call and see which way the conversation went. Maybe she could just have coffee with him and keep it short and sweet. Dinner seemed like more of a commitment to her. If they had coffee and it didn't go well, she was only stuck for an hour or so. She couldn't believe how one short phone message could turn her otherwise quiet, peaceful day into such turmoil. What was the big deal… a cup of coffee shared by two lonely people?

She dialed the number and was hoping he didn't answer, but on the third ring he picked up the phone.

She spoke softly, "Hi Luke, it's Lilli, I was sorry to hear about your father."

Luke started to tell her details about his father. He told her his Dad was now in the Harmorville Rehabilitation Center, right outside of Pittsburgh, getting therapy for his speech and motor skills. The prognosis was good and while his father wanted to return home, he agreed with his stepmother, Arlene, that the facility would serve him better for the next month.

Luke then stated that he only had some undistinguishable green rotting food in his refrigerator and he'd love her to join him for dinner. Without hesitation she agreed. Luke suggested that since it was such a beautiful day would she mind taking a thirty-minute ride to his favorite Italian restaurant, Mario's, way on the outskirts of town. She said she never heard of it before, but it sounded great. He said he would pick her up at five. She then lied and told him she had to go to her daughter's house to babysit for a while, but if he gave her directions, she would meet him there at five thirty. There was no way she could or would get into a car with Luke with all her neighbors watching. Lilli thought she had it all figured out, if they ate by seven, she would be home right at dark.

She found the little restaurant with its neon sign flashing Mario's Italian Ristorante in red, white and green. The building was a small, friendly looking cottage with a gravel parking lot. There were lots of purple cabbage plants lining the walkway to the door of the restaurant. Once Lilli stepped inside, she was met by a very handsome gentleman who spoke with a thick Italian accent. She told him she was going to meet someone, and he immediately pointed her towards Luke's table. The owner of the establishment, Mario, seemed to be very friendly towards Luke. As soon as Luke saw her, he stood up to greet her.

She mentioned to him, "The host seems to know you very well. Do you come here often?"

Luke smiled, "I have been coming to this restaurant every Sunday since I moved to Summerville."

She told him, "I have lived in Summerville all my life and never knew this place existed—how did you find it? It is so out of the way."

He confessed that out of boredom he would drive around and look for interesting places to explore and eat. Once he found Mario's, he was hooked, and he knew she would be too as soon as she tasted Vito's cooking. Luke told her that Vito was Mario's son. Their waiter came to the table and Luke introduced Lilli to Anthony, Mario's grandson. Lilli ordered a glass of Chianti and Luke ordered a club soda.

Luke told her, "By now I think you probably guessed that this is a family run establishment."

They both laughed and then Lilli asked, "Are there any women involved in this family?"

Luke told her that Mario's wife Gia was usually here, but tonight she was visiting her relatives in New York. Lilli told him she was impressed that he knew all of this. Luke said Italians are such warm people and love to share their lives with lonely strangers. He confessed that he would sit and listen to all the stories Mario told him on his many solo visits to the restaurant.

Luke said, "I always longed to have a close family, but it wasn't in the cards for me, so I enjoy hearing about Mario's family."

That was the opening Lilli needed to ask him about his own family.

Luke confessed, "My mother was the only warm spot in my life and when she died, that light went out of my life forever. I like to think that my father did the best he could but for a young child, it just wasn't enough. Once my father married Arlene, it was downhill for me from there. I left for school and then went right on to college and never really looked back."

Lilli stared at him with sadness in her eyes, "I'm sorry you had such a lonely childhood. No child should grow up without its mother."

"I don't dwell on it as much anymore, the past is gone and buried, like my Mom."

"Southerners love to live in the past. The past is the history they made, and they love to share it with anyone who will listen, and if it wasn't such a good story, they'd spin it and turn it until it sounded good anyway."

Luke laughed out loud, and he asked her about her past and then something came over Lilli and she just started to talk as if she was in a trance.

She told him, "I had a wonderful life with my husband of thirty-five years. He treated me like a queen and I hope he knew he was a king among men. I have three wonderful daughters, three great sons-in-law, and the loves of my life are my six grandbabies."

When she was finished, Luke looked over at her and said, "By the look in your eyes and the tenderness in your voice as you spoke about your history, I know you didn't spin one word of it to make it sound better. It came right up from your soul. It's a wonderful history."

Lilli smiled and told him that he was nice to say that. Anthony returned with the drinks and Lilli inquired why Luke wasn't drinking.

He told her, "I gave it up cold turkey a few years ago after I woke up one to many times not knowing what I did the night before."

"Do you miss drinking?" she asked.

"Not at all, I feel better not drinking. However, it did take a little too much time for me to realize that."

She told him she was impressed by his perseverance. He said it was much easier than he would have ever imagined. He should have done it a long time ago.

Luke suggested, "Let's toast to southern history," and they raised their glasses.

"In time, you will have stories to share with your own family."

"By my age, everyone would probably agree I should already have history behind me. I am surely classified as one of those confirmed bachelors."

Lilli was hoping he would reveal his age, but he didn't. Lilli and Luke talked nonstop for another thirty minutes. Mario returned to their table to make dinner suggestions. He told them that Vito had just finished baking Osso Bucco, which was delicious. They said they didn't know what it was but if Mario recommended it, then it must be wonderful. Lilli and Luke smiled and got back to talking about their lives, past and present, but never about the future.

Luke confessed to Lilli, "I have never been interested in any sort of job that would confine me to a desk. I love to be outside or traveling somewhere all the time."

She drifted back to thoughts of how Elgin loved to sit behind his big cherry mahogany desk. This man was a direct opposite of Elgin, but at the same time as Elgin, he was enchanting in every way.

Anthony brought out some garlic bread and butter.

Luke told Lilli, "I think the rule about garlic is that if we both eat it, we'll ward off each other's bad garlic breath."

Lilli laughed and said, "I've never heard that, but I love garlic bread, so here it goes." Lilli finished her wine and Anthony asked her if she wanted another one. She said she'd better not because she had a long drive home.

Luke told her, "Next time, I'll pick you up so you can have two glasses of wine."

Lilli smiled and thought to herself, "I don't know if there is going to be a next time."

Next, a salad appeared at their table with a delicious balsamic garlic vinegar dressing on it.

Lilli laughed and said, "We are going to smell like two cloves of garlic. No vampires for us tonight."

Lilli and Luke laughed and started to eat. They finished every bite as they continued to make small talk. Lilli was surprised that there was never a lull in their conversation. These two people, who were from two different worlds, had so much to say and so much to learn from each other.

Lilli admitted, "My husband didn't like to leave the firm for more than five or six days at a time. I didn't mind short vacations because I'm not the greatest of travelers and I hate flying. Our vacations were mostly to the surrounding beaches like Kiawah Island, Hilton Head and Myrtle Beach. We went to Atlanta a couple of times and stayed in Buckhead."

She told him they had the best shopping there and she could never go to Buckhead without a visit to the Lenox Square and Phipps Plaza Malls.

Luke agreed that Buckhead was a great area, "I remember partying there many times, but that was years ago. It seems like another lifetime ago." Luke said he loved to travel and wanted to complete seeing the rest of the states before he died.

Lilli said, "These days I don't mind staying close to home at all. I guess my age is creeping up on me faster than I'd like to admit. I don't want to miss a day without seeing my grandchildren or my girls. Since my husband died, I've learned how precious each day is and how we never know which one is going to be our last."

Luke said, "I envy your ties to your family. Maybe if I had grown up with my mother in my life, I would have formed similar family ties."

Lilli agreed that it is the mom who holds the family together while the dad is out making a career for himself and the good of his family.

Dinner plates came and went, and still they talked. Dessert arrived, and Lilli looked outside and saw the sun was setting fast. Luke noticed a concerned look on her face as she glanced down at her watch.

He asked, "Do you need to go?"

"Ever since Elgin died, I haven't driven once the sun has set," she admitted. "Since the accident I've been afraid of being out at night."

He assured her, "Once we finish Mario's homemade cake, I will lead you back to your front door." Lilli felt reassured by him and they continued to talk and talk and talk. The next time Lilli glanced at her watch it was nine-thirty.

Lilli said, "I hate to breakup this wonderful evening, but I think we'd better start our drive home. My poor dog must be let out soon. You don't have that problem with Snickers."

Luke smiled and paid the check. Then he thanked Mario, his son and grandson and said they'd be back next Sunday.

Mario smiled and told Lilli, "My wife Gia will be home from New York next week and I can't wait for you to meet her."

Lilli just smiled but didn't commit to anything.

Luke opened Lilli's car door and told her, "Just follow me back down the hill and then before you know it, we'll be back on the main road into Summerville. I'll drive slowly and not lose sight of you."

Lilli smiled and told him, "I want to thank you for a lovely evening and the best food I've tasted in a long time. I'll be okay driving and once we get back into Summerville you can go home, and I'll proceed the few extra miles to my house."

Luke replied quite firmly, "Lilli I'm going to lead you right to your front door. I want to make sure that you are tucked inside safe and sound."

Lilli insisted that wasn't necessary, but Luke wouldn't relent until she agreed. She gave him her address and he said he knew exactly what neighborhood that was. The ride home was scary at first for Lilli but then she put on the radio and listened to the call-in request love line show, and it seemed to relax her. The music was mellow and made her smile. She thought of the evening she had just spent with Luke and wondered if he really meant it when he told Mario they would return to the restaurant next Sunday. Was he just being polite? Did he really want her to join him again? They already had a non-stop talk marathon. What could they possibly have to say to each other next week?

As they neared the entrance to the gated community, Lilli was hoping that Jenn and William were sleeping by now. If they saw Luke pull up in front of her house, she knew the phone would be ringing before she closed her garage door. Luke stopped in front of the mailbox and Lilli pulled into the garage. She thanked him for leading her home.

He said, "This was by far the best Sunday I've had since I moved into Summerville."

"I've had a lovely time, too."

"Okay, so since we both agree it was a good time, we have to have a replay next Sunday. I'll pick you up at six."

Lilli quickly dissuaded him about picking her up, and then she couldn't believe the words that flew out of her mouth next, "I'll meet you at Southlake Shopping Center at six next Sunday."

She went into the house and sat down on the bench in the mudroom and talked aloud to her dog who was now begging to go out. "Gigi, I think I might have made a big mistake tonight."

After walking the dog, Lilli turned out the lights and walked upstairs with her little companion following closely at her heels. The phone rang, and Lilli dreaded to answer it, in fear that Jenn and William had seen Luke's car in front of the house. What lie could she make up so they would believe her? It turned out that it was her daughter Noelle saying that she was worried about her. She had called earlier to check on her and there was no answer. She just knew Lilli wouldn't go out at night. Lilli told her that her friend from church, Rhonda, picked her up and they went to dinner and a movie. Noelle was happy to hear that Lilli went out. Lilli knew that she couldn't tell anyone that she went out with Luke. She didn't want anyone to agree with her that she was an old fool. What would her daughters think of her? They never talked about her seeing anyone. They would never accept anyone after Elgin.

Chapter 14

Lilli tossed and turned as the night wore on. She had such mixed emotions of acting like an old fool while at the same time feeling happy and excited for the first time in over two years. The morning light came into the room and Lilli jumped out of bed, put the coffee pot on, and took the dog for a walk. Then the spring in her step came to a crashing halt. She saw her next-door neighbor, Jenn, getting her newspaper from the mailbox holder. They exchanged good mornings and Lilli held her breath. Jenn asked her how she was doing, and Lilli said fine and to Lilli's relief the conversation came to a quick end. Lilli was convinced that Jenn or William didn't see Luke's car last night. The question about a strange car on Lilli's driveway would have been the first thing out of Jenn's mouth. Lilli retreated into the house, had a cup of coffee, a bowl of cereal, read the newspaper and then went upstairs to shower. When she was finished, she started to put on her makeup when the phone rang. She sat on the bed as she answered the phone. It was Savannah Grace. She wanted to know if Lilli had any plans for the day.

"Nothing, in particular, what do you have in mind?" Lilli responded.

"I just wanted to know if you wanted to go to lunch later. Since the club was closed, we could go into town to the new little café that's just opened. I don't remember the name of it but I've heard that it's wonderful," Savannah exclaimed.

"Why not? Pick me up at noon." Lilli decided.

As she continued to get dressed, she noticed that her hair was a little lifeless and she could use a little lift with either a haircut or maybe some highlights. She would ask Savannah's opinion on how she could go about sprucing herself up.

Savannah pulled up exactly at noon. She prided herself on her ability to always be on time or even a little early. Lilli walked to the car with a smile on her face.

Savannah asked, "Why are you smiling like the Cheshire cat who's just caught a mouse?"

Lilli laughed, "Can't I smile on this lovely day, with the Carolina blue sky shining above?"

As they drove towards town, Lilli told Savannah that she was tired of her twenty-year-old hairdo and could she recommend a new style for her.

Savannah looked at her strangely and asked her straight out, "What's going on with you Lilli Belle Jackson?"

Lilli denied there was anything going on, "I just need to get out of my rut and get back into life."

Savannah agreed and said they should go to the salon after lunch and ask Inger for a new do.

During lunch, Lilli seemed to have a new attitude. She rambled on about silly things and giggled like a schoolgirl. After lunch they went into Inger's and Inger ran up and welcomed Lilli back with a great big hug and kiss. Lilli confessed that she was dyeing her own hair and since her hair grew at a snail's pace, there was no reason to come in for a haircut till now.

Savannah stated, "Lilli wants a new look. She needs something to match her new attitude."

Inger smiled sweetly, "Y'all look through those magazines and try to narroh' it down a bit more for me."

Finally, after Lilli and Savannah thumbed through four or five magazines, they came to a hairstyle that both of them thought might look good on Lilli. They brought the picture over to Inger and after looking at the picture and pulling Lilli's hair toward her cheeks, Inger said, "I think that you have the perfect oval shaped face that would work well with this inverted wedge style. Have a sit in my chair and let's get started."

Inger got to work, first she colored Lilli's hair, highlighted it. and then started to cut it and as Savannah was getting her nails polished as she watched Lilli's transformation, "I really like the new Lilli. I think I'm getting a tad bit jealous of how young Lilli's looking. Inger can you give me a younger look like Lilli's next week?"

Inger told her, "Certainly dear, you set up a time next week and we'll go for it!"

When they left the salon, Lilli was very happy with the results of her new look.

Savannah told her, "The next thing you need is some new

makeup."

Lilli popped up quickly and said, "One major adjustment at a time please, Savannah. This hairdo is going to take a little getting used to. Wait until my girls see the new me, they are going to think I've lost it for sure."

On the way home, Savannah asked, "Lilli, do you want to join us Saturday night at the club for dinner?"

For the first time Lilli agreed to go to the couples Saturday night formal dinner. Savannah's mouth fell open because she never thought Lilli would accept the invitation that she has extended to her religiously every week, for the past year and a half. Both women seemed excited about it.

Chapter 15

Once Lilli got home, she looked at herself in the mirror and admired her hair and her look in general. She knew deep inside her that it was Luke that was making a difference in her. In a low whisper that was just audible she said, "Elgin, please be happy for me." Then she thought to herself how Elgin was the love of her life and how he would always hold the largest place in her heart. She knew she had to love again, or she might as well have died with him in the accident. Then suddenly out of nowhere, she remembered one conversation they had at the club one Saturday night with Savannah and the gang. The gossip at the club centered around the widow Elle, who was getting married to a younger man. Most of Elgin's friends said they didn't want their wives to remarry and give all their hard-earned money to a new boy toy. They said they would come back and make their wives miserable if they tried that.

Elgin said, "I give her credit for going on with her life. It is a sort of tribute to the good marriage she once had with Matt. She just wants to recapture some normalcy in her life. Since it can't be with Matt, it might as well be with someone else, why not a younger man? Why should she take care of an old man? Let some young buck take care of her." He then smiled and looked over at Lilli and told her if he ever died, he wanted her to find some young stud and enjoy herself.

Everyone at the table laughed out loud and Lilli said, "Okay, if you insist, Elgin."

Elgin continued, "Life is for the living and we should all enjoy it for as long as we can."

It was so uncanny that Elgin made that little speech to Lilli and his friends and in less than a month, all these people would be standing at his gravesite. Lilli wondered if Elgin had a premonition about his life coming to an end.

Saturday night rolled around, and Lilli slipped into Elgin's favorite little black dress. He would always tell her that she looked very smart and simply elegant in it. Tonight, she would show up at the club as she did so many Saturday nights in the past. Only this night she wouldn't have Elgin to dance with or to whisper silly jokes to her. While she was sad, she was also happy because she was doing exactly what Elgin had told her to do, "LIVE LIFE!"

The doorbell rang and Brian, Savannah Grace's husband, stood there and just stared at Lilli for a moment. He told Lilli that he loved her new hair style and she looked great in that dress. Lilli surmised that Savannah gave him a heads up about her hairdo. He then helped Lilli on with her coat just as Elgin used to do.

When they arrived at the club, all the regulars were already sitting at the table. The men got up and greeted the three of them. Both Anna Lee's husband, Kevin, and Carol Ann's husband, Bill, commented on how lovely Lilli looked. They told her they were glad to see her and hoped she would continue to join them on Saturday nights. Lilli smiled and then caught a glance of Luke crossing the edge of the dining room on his way downstairs to the locker rooms. Lilli ordered a drink and then told her friends she had to go to the ladies' room and would be back in a few minutes. Lilli made her way down to the ladies' locker room with the hope of seeing Luke. She couldn't find him in the hallway or the pro shop, so she started up the stairs and turned as she heard a familiar voice say, "Good evening, Mrs. Jackson." She turned on the stairs and wobbled by the speed of her turn and Luke lunged forward to save her from a fall. She composed herself and they smiled at each other.

Luke told her, "Wow! I love your new hairstyle. You look terrific in that dress."

Lilli felt her cheeks start to flush and she thanked him and said she was glad she ran into him. "I was thinking about you and the lovely time I had last Sunday at Mario's."

Luke jumped in, "You haven't changed your mind about going back again tomorrow night?"

She assured him she hadn't changed her mind and reminded him that she'd leave her car behind the Southlake Shopping Center on the way out of town. He said it was no problem to pick her up but she insisted and he knew why. She was afraid of being seen with him in her neighborhood.

The night went by quickly as Lilli fell back into the same scene, she had visited so many times with Elgin. She danced with Brian and Bill and had a good time even though she knew they were pity dances.

When the last round of drinks came, Bill raised his glass and said, "This drink is for our old friend Elgin who is gone now but will never be forgotten."

Lilli's eyes filled with tears. She knew she would always love Elgin and always smile at the mention of his name, but still she had to admit that Luke had sparked something in her that was already far more than she wanted it to be.

Lilli got home around 1 a.m. and thought of all the other couples' nights when she returned home with Elgin and how they would make love. He was the only man she had ever been with. Just the same, she knew he was a wonderful lover who made her feel special every time they had been together sexually. She didn't know if she could ever go to bed with Luke—she hoped he didn't expect her to. Besides, how could she ever forget the one true love of her life. She was petrified that Luke's presence in her life would somehow overshadow the memories of Elgin. She liked her relationship with Luke now just the way it was, a nice dinner and easy conversation to help pass the long nights. She prayed that Luke wouldn't tire of her yet. After all, he was a man and would expect her to take their relationship to the next level soon. She knew that men could go to bed without loving a woman, but she wouldn't do that. How could she do that to herself, or to her Elgin? What had she gotten herself into?

Chapter 16

Sunday started with a phone call from Lilli's daughter Tammy inviting her over for dinner. She made up an excuse why she couldn't attend. She told her daughter that she was talked into going to a Bunco night with her friends from church, Doreen and Donna. Tammy said it would be good for her to get out with other women her own age. They would get together during the week for dinner. Lilli hated to lie but she just couldn't tell anyone the truth right now. She thought to herself that this thing with Luke would probably be ending soon so why deal with all the disapproving looks and heavy conversations now.

Lilli pulled into the Southlake Shopping Center at 4:45 p.m. and to her surprise Luke was already there. She stepped out of her car, locked it, and walked towards Luke's car. She never really noticed what kind of car he had before, she only knew that it was red. Now she noted it was a mustang convertible. Even though the car was spotless and in real good shape, she could tell it wasn't new.

Lilli looked delighted, "I thought I would be the early one and be waiting for you."

He said, "I got here about a half hour ago."

She smiled at him and told him, "I always liked to be a little early, but never a half hour early."

"I didn't want you waiting alone in a deserted parking lot," he said lovingly.

"That's very considerate. Thank you."

As they made their way down the windy roads towards Mario's, they were never at a loss for words. They talked about the club, his tennis lessons, their animals, and it all seemed so interesting. Luke had a great sense of humor and made a lot of funny comments. They were still laughing as they pulled into the parking lot. Mario met them at the door again and this time introduced Lilli to his wife Gia. The two women talked for a few minutes then they went to the same booth that they sat in last Sunday. It was so comfortable being there with Luke. Luke asked her if she had a good time at the couple's dinner dance last night.

Lilli confessed, "It was the first time I've been there since my husband has died. At first, I was a little bit uncomfortable, but by the end of the night I was okay with it. Maybe it was the wine that made me relax."

Luke reminded her that she looked stunning in her black dress and new look. She then mentioned how all of her girlfriends' husbands danced with her.

"I know before they got to the club those poor men had schooling from their wives to make sure that I wasn't a wall flower all night. In all the years I've been at the club it was the first time I ever danced with all my friends' husbands in one night," Lilli giggled.

Once again, they didn't have to order, and the most delicious food was brought to their table. As they ate their chicken saltimbocca, Luke disclosed about being lonely ever since he was a child. "How is it that now as I'm nearing my forty-eighth birthday, I wished I had a wife and child of my own to share my life with?"

Lilli told him, "Men can have children way up into their fifties and sixties. It isn't too late for you."

Luke shrugged in disagreement, and then it was dessert time.

Lilli glanced at her watch and it was already nine-thirty. She wondered where had the time gone again.

Luke said, "Our two dinner dates have flown by too quickly. Now I have to wait till next Sunday to have a good time again."

Lilli blushed.

Luke leaned into her and whispered, "Your cheeks look a little flushed."

"Wine always does that to me," she stated with a flair, waving her hands in the air as if to bring some cool air down to her to relieve her of her glowing iridescence.

Mario and Gia appeared at their table with two glasses of Sambuca, they told them it was an after-dinner drink that tasted like licorice. Lilli took the glass off the tray, but Luke refused his. Lilli noticed that there were three coffee beans in the glass and asked the significance of that. Mario told her it was an Italian thing and it stood for the Father, Son and Holy Ghost. Luke and Lilli laughed, as she tasted the Sambuca. She admitted that it was good and wondered why she never heard of this cordial before. Mario told her it was an old Italian liquor, but most bars just started to carry it a few years ago when it became trendy. Lilli swallowed her Sambuca down very slowly. Luke watched her and thought how delicate and classy she was. Luke continued talking as Lilli sipped her drink and he found himself speaking much too rapidly. He realized that he was rambling on like an old biddy. He couldn't understand what had come over him. By the time Anthony delivered the check and Luke paid the bill it was nearing ten o'clock.

Lilli couldn't believe the time and as they left the restaurant Luke told her, "Once again, I've had a great time, can we do it again next week? This is the only thing I look forward to all week."

Lilli said, "I had a wonderful time, too and I would love to do it again."

Excited, he said, "It's a date then. Next Sunday, I'll pick you up at the same time, same place."

The date was set.

For the next 10 months, they met every Sunday for dinner.

Chapter 17

As they were walking to the car, he had finally gotten up the nerve to tell her, "I love you Lilli and I know you're right for me. If you need more time to adjust to us as a couple, I'll understand and give you all the time you need."

Lilli took a deep breath and to her own amazement, she responded, "While you can't replace what I had with Elgin for thirty-five years, I must admit that you do make me smile again, and fill a big hole in my heart."

Luke asserted, "That's the best place to start then, with your heart."

"Ever since Elgin died, I've been frightened about everything from driving at night to sleeping in the dark. For over two years, I pulled back from life, but once you entered my world, I knew I had to rejoin the living and just couldn't sit on the sidelines anymore."

Luke declared, "I want to be there for you. I've never wanted to be this attached to anyone, but here I am wanting you. I want to be the one to hold you when you're frightened. If you fall, I want to pick you up."

Lilli just stood there silently for a minute while this soaked in, and then told Luke, "I feel the same way, but I'm not sure if we could have a serious relationship right now."

Luke stared at her lovingly, "Lilli, I'm in no rush but it's been over two years since Elgin died. You loved him for thirty-five years, but he's gone now. You and I have a chance to love each other now, please don't let it slip by."

Lilli told Luke it was a big decision and she would have to think it over. She thought to herself, how would her daughters take the news of their mother dating a much younger man. How would her friends from the club react when they heard that Luke, her tennis coach, was now her boyfriend?

Luke broke into the thoughts swirling around her head when he said, "As long as I can put that incredible smile on your face each day, I'll be a happy man. I know you're right for me. You make me happy, something I never thought I could be."

Lilli admitted to Luke that when Elgin died, she was ready to die also, but now she was glad that she didn't. She is no longer scared to live, and she doesn't want to hug her pillow at night anymore. He told her to get in the car, and when he got inside, he leaned over to her. His kiss was soft and long, and Lilli was shocked by the way she reacted to him. For a brief second, she started to put on the brakes, but Luke could feel the passion hidden behind her cautious kiss so he didn't stop. He kissed her again and it was with such passion. She thought she'd be afraid of kissing him since the only man she'd ever been with was Elgin. After they kissed, she knew it was right. Luke's touch was much different than Elgin's. Elgin's was home for her, but Luke was a little on the edgy side, more intense. The newness of this Lilli found very exciting. Lilli had to finally admit to herself that she was more than a little attracted by Luke's touch.

Luke asked her, "Can I come home with you?"

She nervously replied, "That wouldn't be a good idea."

She knew she couldn't make love to him in Elgin's bed. She told him that she couldn't go home with him either. Gigi was alone for more than five hours already and had to be taken on her nightly walk.

Luke suggested, "Let's swing by your house and pick up your dog and take her to my apartment."

When Lilli put a quick end to that idea Luke asked, "Are you looking for an excuse not to be with me?"

She assured him that wasn't the case, but it would just take a little planning before they could be together. She didn't want to sneak around and make their relationship seem like a dirty little secret. She would have to break the news to her daughters first, and this would have to be done slowly and gently. She didn't want to hurt them.

Luke questioned her, "How can it hurt them, love never hurts Lilli, it's not being loved that hurts?"

Lilli responded softly, "I, I need some time to sort things out."

"I'll give you all the time you need Lilli, but just know I am sure this is right for the both of us."

Lilli thought about it for a few minutes and then she suggested,

"Let's try to arrange a get-a-way to the beach. I will tell my daughters on Friday at dinner."

Luke leaned over to her and kissed her gently on her cheek. Lilli then leaned into him and kissed him hard. She surprised herself at how she was feeling. Lilli held Luke's hand on the drive back to town. When they got to her car, he walked her over and opened the door. He grabbed her once again and pressed hard against her. She could feel that he was getting aroused, so she pulled away slowly. They kissed one last time and he helped her into her car. She rolled down her window and he said he would follow her home.

Chapter 18

Lilli lay awake most of the night. The conversations she had with Luke swirled around her head for hours. How would she tell her girls about Luke? What would her friends say? Would they all be talking behind her back as they did about Elle? Would their friendly kisses turn to claws? She had to call her cousin Phyllis and confide in her before she went crazy. This secret was just too big to keep to herself. She knew that Phyllis would keep her secret and even help her figure out her next move. Once she made up her mind to take this first step, she fell asleep.

With the loss of Elgin, Lilli had learned that there was no real security on this earth, only opportunity. She was determined to grab this opportunity with Luke or her soul would surely die forever. Lilli knew that she didn't want to regret giving up a life with Luke. Her next test of courage would be to love Luke openly. She knew that she would have to live with her choices despite the resounding criticism that was surely headed her way. She remembers her Mom telling her, "In the darkest of times there is no medicine like hope." For the first time in over two years she felt like there was some hope in her life.

Lilli called Phyllis the next morning before nine, which is something she would normally never do. Southern women have the unspoken nine o'clock call rule…don't call before 9 a.m. or after 9 p.m. Today was different. Lilli could tell that she woke her cousin up, but she knew once Phyllis heard this news, she would be wide awake in a New York minute.

She told her, "I don't know where to start, Phyllis."

Alarmed, Phyllis asked, "Oh, no, what's wrong Lilli, you never call me this early?"

She replied gleefully, "For the first time in over two years everything is fine, nothing is wrong, can you believe it?"

"You woke me up to tell me you are fine?"

Lilli laughed and then she started to tell Phyllis that Luke had entered her life through a door that she thought was closed forever. Phyllis and Lilli talked for near an hour and by the end of the conversation, Lilli knew she had told the right person first. It wasn't only that Phyllis had agreed with her in her choice to live and love again, but she said it loud and clear, "just go for it." It was the fact that Phyllis told her, "Elgin is smiling down and giving you his blessing." Lilli told her that she hoped her girls would give their blessing, but she had her doubts.

Phyllis said, "I know how important your family is to you Lilli Belle, but this has nothing to do with them. After all, they are living their own lives and you should have that same chance."

They exchanged good-byes and Lilli hung up the phone with a vivacious grin.

The next one she would call would be Savannah Grace. Her phone was busy, so Lilli hung up with a sigh of relief. Her relief was short lived because within the next five minutes she was telling Savannah that Luke and she were more than just friends.

Savannah said, "I was tellin' Tina and Irene that somethin' was different about you, but never in my wildest dreams would I have thought it had to anything to do with Luke…the tennis pro!"

Lilli explained how they first started seeing each other and then how what started as a friendship had ended in this new love.

Savannah asked, "Lilli, are you sure it's love and not just a way of fending off the loneliness for the both of you?"

Lilli declared, "If that's what you want to think, so be it Savannah."

Savannah asked, "Have you gone to bed with him?"

Lilli told her the truth, "Not yet."

Savannah said that she had to get off the phone to digest this news for a while and would call her back before lunch. Lilli knew that Savannah Grace was very skeptical of men ever since her husband, Brian, had that brief affair with his slut hairdresser, Martha. Savannah said that Brian was just like all men going through their forties with his mid-life crisis. Lilli and Elgin knew that was Savannah's way of saving face. However, through little comments that Savannah would make, and the very short leash that Brian was on they all still knew that she didn't forgive or trust Brian. Lilli did some chores around the house and kept practicing monologues for her girls about how right it is to have Luke in her life.

She devised a plan to tell her daughters Friday night at dinner at her house. She would ask the girls to come over, but to get babysitters, so it could be an adult dinner. She wanted to speak to them without the little ones listening in. Jeanne was a little inquisitive as to why the children weren't invited because her mom never excluded them from anything. Lilli told her that they just needed an adult night this Friday. Jeanne still wasn't convinced but when she saw it was futile to continue to ask why, she gave up.

Savannah Grace called back by noon and started rattling off what seemed like a prepared summation of the why nots. She was sure that it was a mistake for Lilli to take up with Luke.

Lilli asked, "Why is it a mistake when he makes me happy, and I can finally smile again, what could be wrong with that?"

Savannah continued without taking a breath, "We know nothing of him and maybe he's just after your money and status in the community. Maybe he has some secret life that no one knows about. In one leap he would go from tennis pro in the country club to a class A club member in good standing."

Lilli broke in when Savannah was taking a deep breath, "For the last six months I have found out everything I need to know about Luke. I know that he is a wonderful man with a kind heart. My dad always said, 'A man is measured in two ways, one by his family and the other by his word.' Luke doesn't have a family to speak of, but I believe he is a man of his word. He is not trying to get my money or status into the club."

Savannah couldn't believe that Lilli had kept this secret from her. Next came the question that she knew everyone would be concerned with, "What about your age difference?"

Lilli said, "What about it, does it bother you? It doesn't mean anything to us. Luke makes me happy and brings a smile to my face and that is what Elgin would want for me." She assured Savannah that she didn't need her blessing and she just wanted to tell her before the gossip got out.

Savannah rambled on further, "Lilli, what do the girls think about this situation?"

Lilli told her they would find out this Friday. She asked Savannah to keep it under wraps until then. Savannah promised she would and asked if she could tell Brian.

Lilli said, "I always told Elgin everything, so just tell Brian to keep it quiet for a few more days." Lilli hung up the phone and said to herself, "Well that went rather well" and smiled. She was determined not to make anyone bring her down. She wouldn't give anyone her consent to make her feel unhappy and wrong in this decision.

Luke called. She told him that she told Phyllis and Savannah and would be telling her children in a few days.

He said, "I knew that Savannah would react like that, but it's okay. Don't be hurt because basically she is just trying to protect you."

Lilli replied, "It really doesn't matter what any of my friends think, it's just my three girls whose feelings I am most anxious about. I don't want them to think that I am dishonoring their father or the life we once shared." She told Luke that on many occasions in conversations when people died, Elgin told the children that he would want me to find someone if anything happened to him.

He said, "He wouldn't want me to be alone in my golden years." He would always follow that with, "But let's hope that doesn't happen any time soon."

Luke laughed and said, "I think Elgin and I would have gotten along very well."

Lilli told him, "I'm sure of it."

Chapter 19

Friday arrived much sooner than Lilli wished. She had butterflies in her stomach, but at the same time, the anticipation gave her an adrenalin rush that she hadn't felt in a long time. The girls arrived one right after another around six. Lilli had arranged the bar with everyone's favorite drinks. The boys, as Elgin would call them, went to the bar and made the cocktails. Carlton made two cosmopolitans, one for Noelle and one for Tammy. Jamie asked Lilli if she wanted a glass of wine, which she willingly accepted. Lilli thought to herself, "False courage, oh hell, whatever it takes to get through this night." Jamie gave one glass of wine to Jeanne and one to Lilli. The girls knew something was up, but with all their speculation they never in their quest for the meaning of this grown-up dinner ever would have imagined that their mom had a "boyfriend."

Lilli made a joke, "Do we eat first or talk first?"

Of course, the girls said in unison, "Talk, tell us what's going on."

Noelle added, "You're scaring us."

Lilli assured them there was nothing to be afraid of. As Lilli was nearing the end of her wine, Dana poured her another one. Her cheeks were now getting flush. She didn't know if it was the wine or her nerves. Everyone could always tell when Lilli had two glasses of wine. Elgin's joke was that Lilli was a cheap date, two glasses of wine and straight to sleep.

Lilli got right to it and told the girls that she was seeing a man. At first, the girls tried to smile, and guess which widower it was from the club.

"Or even better," Tammy asked, "is it Uncle Steve?"

Lilli told them they didn't know this gentleman. The questions came hot and heavy now. Noelle's journalism background kicked into high gear. Who, what, when, where and how? Lilli told them to all quiet down. "I will answer all your questions as soon as I explain the whole story to you."

Lilli started at the beginning with her tennis lessons and then the chance veterinary meeting and finally her many Sunday dinners and long phone calls. Lilli did tell them that he was forty-eight years old. With this admission, the girls started shooting each other looks. Finally, Lilli finished filling them in on Luke's past and present.

Everyone sat there quietly digesting this information when finally, the silence was broken when Carlton was the first to speak, "I think it's great that you've found someone to spend time with. You shouldn't be alone. You shouldn't spend lonely evenings in this big house. I don't care how young he is, if you are happy, I know Dad would want you to continue on with your life and be happy."

With those comments, Noelle gave Carlton her famous death look, so he kept quiet after that.

Noelle stated emphatically, "You should have chosen someone in your own social circle."

Lilli was just as emphatic, "Dad and I didn't raise you to be a snob."

Noelle continued her interrogation, "Did you do a background check on this man?"

"Don't be ridiculous, Noelle," Lilli retorted.

Lilli was waiting for the other shoe to drop and was getting a little nervous because both Tammy and Jeanne hadn't said much yet. She turned to Jeanne and asked her what she thought.

Jeanne expressed her concerns about Luke's history. "Do you really know all there is to know about this tennis pro?"

Lilli was a little offended and said, "His name is Luke."

Lilli then looked over at Tammy as she remarked, "This is quite a shock and I have to think about this for a while before I voice any opinions." Tammy then added, "I am glad you aren't as sad anymore, but I don't want this man to replace Dad."

"Remember Tammy, I loved your Dad all his life and I will miss him the rest of mine."

Lilli assured her, "Death ends a life, but not a relationship. Your Dad will forever be special to me and can never be replaced by anyone. He held my heart for thirty-five years and how dare any of you think he won't forever remain there until the day I die."

Lilli's eyes welled up with tears.

She clutched her chest and said, "The tragedy of losing Dad had pierced a hole through my heart and for more than two years I was bleeding to death slowly each day. Now it's time to stop the pain and heal the hole. I can only do this through living again."

Tammy apologized, reached out to her and stated, "This has come as a big shock to me. Mom, you know that I am the daughter that doesn't handle change well."

Lilli continued, "Dad wouldn't want me to be alone to live out the rest of my life with only his dog as a companion. I am sure that he would approve, and once you have all met Luke, I'm sure all your fears will be set aside, and you will approve, too. Of course, he could never take Dad's place, for a while there, I was more afraid of life than death, and death was starting to look like a way out for me. I don't feel that way anymore."

They all agreed that they wanted her to be happy, but Noelle exclaimed, "We had no idea that you were seeing anyone, and we have to get use to the idea of you having someone else in your life besides Dad."

Jeanne asked if anyone else knew about Luke. Lilli told them that Phyllis and Savannah Grace found out about Luke a few days ago. "What did they have to say? Were they shocked?"

"Well, like all of you, they were totally shocked. Phyllis was truly happy for me while I fear that Savannah is worried about my reputation. I told her that I'm only concerned about my character because that is who I really am, and my reputation is only what others think I am. Until she walks in my shoes, she can't judge me."

Lilli confided to them that no one was more shocked than she was when she realized she had these feelings for Luke. She wiped away her tears and said, "I'm really happy now, all I ask is that you be happy for me, too."

After a very long hour of cocktails and inquiry, Lilli asked if any of them had an appetite.

"I have prepared another of your Dad's favorite dinners - filet mignon, twice baked potatoes and creamed spinach."

Her family all got up and gathered around the dinner table. Lilli brought the food to the table and everyone ate, but there was a noticeably quieter group gathered at the Jackson dinner table this hour. Lilli served dessert, another of Elgin's favorite, rice pudding and told them that she prepared all of Dad's favorites on purpose tonight.

"He is with me every day. I have my memories of us as a couple and a family and they will never fade, but I must move forward with my life. A few years ago, I was unsure of my place in this world but now with Luke I've found a reason to hope again. I really have been given a second chance. While I was mourning Dad, everyday I'd remember something I forgot to say to him. Something I didn't do for him and it hurt me so much. I don't ever want to have such regrets again. I don't want any more what if's, or I should haves. I can't let this chance pass me by. The love we find in our lives is the only single true thing we will ever ex-perience. I was so lucky to experience it with Dad and now twice blessed to have Luke. I've learned that the hardest thing in life is to decide which bridge to cross and which to burn. If I'm willing to take this chance, then you should all be willing to take it with me."

The girls were all teared up now, but at the same time they managed a smile for their mother. They knew that their mother would always love their Dad, but now she had to finally say good-bye to him in a way they never expected. The next thing Tammy said was that she would like to meet Luke. Lilli told her she would arrange a dinner for all of them to meet Luke in a few weeks.

Noelle asked Lilli is she was planning to marry Luke and Lilli looked at her three daughters and said, "My future is uncertain, and it's just one day at a time now." She honestly had no answer for them concerning marriage. She felt they all needed time to adjust to this new situation, even her.

Jeanne said, "How do I explain Luke to Gabby? She was so attached to Dad and still misses him an awful lot."

Lilli said she was sure that Gabby would handle it better than the rest of them.

Lilli kissed them all goodnight as they were leaving and then took Gigi for a quick walk. While outside, she gazed up into the sky that was lit up with diamonds and a big bright moon. She talked to Elgin for a few minutes and asked him for a sign about Luke. When she returned inside, the phone was ringing, and it was Luke.

Lilli told Luke that her confession to her kids about the two of them went as well as could be expected. "After all, it was a complete and total shock." She also said that the boys were okay with it, but Elgin wasn't their Dad. The girls had to have a few days to wrap their minds around this strange idea of their mother with a new man.

Luke said he understood perfectly and was looking forward to meeting them.

"I think they need a few weeks," said Lilli. First, we have to plan our own special weekend."

Luke said, "Next weekend will work for me, how about you?"

She said it was fine. Lilli joked with Luke and said, "I hope this halo I've worn for my family for many years doesn't slip down a few inches and become my noose."

Luke laughed and told Lilli, "No matter what anyone thinks of you, to me you'll always be an angel." They said their goodnights and Lilli and Gigi went upstairs and got ready for bed.

Surprisingly, Lilli slept very soundly. She woke up around eight to the sounds of the neighborhood. Lilli's routine never varied much but this day with the release of her secret, she felt like she was gliding on air as she prepared her morning tea and breakfast. She smiled as she walked the dog and collected the newspaper. She sang in the shower, something that she hadn't done in a long time. Life now seemed new again, like she was in love for the first time all over again.

Savannah Grace called her to find out how the night with the girls went. Lilli assured her that the girls would be fine with a little adjustment period. Phyllis called next to find out if Lilli was okay. She said she hadn't felt this good in over two years. Phyllis was genuinely happy for her. They made a date to get together soon.

Next, Luke called to see how Lilli slept and she told him she hasn't slept so soundly in a long time. He said he was worried about her, but she assured him there was nothing to be worried about.

Lilli said "Luke, when Elgin died my heart was broken into a hundred little pieces, but through it all it kept beating. Sometimes I couldn't understand how it could continue to beat through all the pain I was feeling but it did. Most days it even hurt to breathe. Now I know it kept beating so I would stay alive to love again. I cried continuously because the sun had gone out of my life, but now with you my tears have dried up and I can see and feel the warmth of the sun once more. Luke, can anyone doubt that this relationship is anything but good for me?"

Luke told her he was happy that she was feeling so positive about their future. He reminded her that he had next weekend free and he asked her if they were still on for the beach.

With a smile on her lips Lilli said, "I'm counting down the days until we're together."

Luke asked, "Would you like to go to Mario's tomorrow night?"

Lilli said simply, "Of course, I was counting on it."

Lilli then made a few phone calls of her own to make reservations at a beautiful bed and breakfast seaside resort that she had heard about on Pawley's Island. She knew that they would practically have the place to themselves since the tourist season had come to an end. It was only 90 miles away in case there was a problem at home. Pawley's Island was only four miles long and on this strip of beautiful beachfront there lay a single line of houses all standing in a row. There wasn't a grocery store, marina, or gas station to be had. Lilli thought it sounded perfect for a romantic weekend. Lilli was sure they wouldn't run into anyone that she knew there. She then reserved one of the six private cottages available. She made sure there was an ocean view and it had a king size bed. The proprietors of the Inn seemed very friendly and eager to please. They told Lilli that they offered three meals a day and they had an excellent selection of seafood and low-country cuisine. Lilli told them it sounded wonderful. She asked if they could possibly have champagne and yellow roses in the room upon their arrival next Friday night. They assured her they would have everything she asked for in the cottage waiting for her. Lilli hung up the phone and stayed excited the rest of the day. She started to make tentative plans. First, she would have to get her hair dyed and styled next Friday morning. She would then have to buy a new night gown and slippers. She knew that her underwear would have to be updated also. She had to make sure she packed her Shalimar perfume.

Lilli started to blush as she daydreamed about her upcoming weekend. She was a little wary about telling the girls about her trip. She thought about lying and telling them she was going on another weekend shopping spree with Phyllis to New York. She knew that Phyllis would cover for her. She then thought better of this lie that would grow legs of its own before long, so she decided to tell them straight out. After all, she was a widow who was going to turn fifty-five soon. What was she waiting for? They would have to understand, but would they?

Lilli decided that she wasn't going to let anyone ruin this weekend for her and Luke. She had made up her mind and she was going to follow her heart now. Lilli secretly hoped that the girls would remember what she always preached to them…

"In life, always be a little kinder than necessary because you never know what the other person is going through."

Chapter 20

By mid-week Lilli could put if off no more. She would make her call before she went to bed. She called Noelle first and told her to get Jeanne and Tammy on the phone, so they could have one of their famous conference calls. This would at least save Lilli two calls. She could say it once and they would all hear her at the same time. They were all connected, and Lilli blurted it right out. "I'm going away for the weekend with Luke."

As the poets say often, "The silence was deafening."

She could hear what they were thinking, "How could she do this to Dad, it's too soon; he's just cat fishing her to get her money; he's just a social climber."

Lilli continued and said she was going to cross this bridge into life. "I'm sorry if you are disappointed in me or upset, but I'm doing this for me. You all went on with your lives when Dad died, and it was the right thing to do for you and your families. I was the only one that didn't move on with my life until now. I think I deserve this, I want this. This is my chance to start living again. All I ask of the three of you, is that you don't judge me too harshly. Try to keep an open mind."

Lilli then told them of her plans to go to Pawley's Island Friday night, and she would return Sunday. She assured them that her cell phone would always be on and they could reach her if they needed her. No one was speaking, and this was very unusual, especially for Noelle.

Lilli said, "I guess this is where I say that the cats' got your tongues."

Jeanne chimed in and said, "Don't you think you are moving a little too fast?"

Lilli replied, "For over the last two years I have been in neutral at best, but most of the time in reverse. So, no. It's not fast at all."

Tammy spoke next, "If you think it's the right thing to do, then I will back you, but I did want to meet Luke first."

"I'm only positive of one thing right now," Lilli said softly, "Dad would want me to go on living. He was a realist and always told me that if anything happened to him, he would want me to find someone else and live my life to the fullest. I'm positive I'm not dishonoring him in any way, shape or form. By taking this chance it shows how wonderful my life was with him. If I can recapture any part of that for this last portion of my life, I'm flattering the life we once shared. If we had a bad marriage, I would never take this chance to be with someone else. I can't live with my memories of Dad anymore. I won't live that way." The last thing she said, "Please don't be mad at me. You will meet Luke real soon."

They ended the conversation with polite goodbyes. The last thing she heard was a concerned, "Call us when you get back Sunday."

Lilli called Luke and told him that she just got off the phone with her daughters. She told them that she was going away with him and they were all taken back a little.

Luke comforted her, "Lilli, there was really no warning of us as a couple. Then, this weekend away came up quickly so, of course, they were shocked. Just be patient with them."

She answered, "I'm not mad or even disappointed, and I know as soon as they meet you they will come around."

Luke wondered if he should have met them before they went away for the weekend. Lilli assured him that she was sure they were doing the right thing.

Lilli said goodnight and went to bed shortly after she hung up the phone with Luke. She had a restless night and tossed in her bed until daylight. As she was dozing, she felt herself smile. She awoke to the feeling that someone had just kissed her lips. It took her breath away for a moment. She bolted straight up in bed and touched her lips. Was she dreaming? She felt tears streaming down her cheeks and ran to the bathroom to look in the mirror. The tears were real. The kiss was, too. Lilli returned to her bed and sat on the edge of the bed for a long time. Was Elgin giving her a last goodbye kiss, a sign to move on now? Did she just imagine all of this? She decided it was Elgin giving her the ok to move forward with her life. She knew she would never tell anyone about this kiss. This was the last thing between her and Elgin. Elgin was her guardian angel now.

The rest of the week flew by and finally the day had arrived. Lilli had lots of fears about herself as a lover. With Elgin, their lovemaking was so familiar and easy, they had gained a rhythm over the years that only comes with loving someone for so long. She wondered if it would ever be that way with Luke. Would they ever get that chance to find out or would this be their beginning and their end? What if he expected more than she could give him? After Elgin, what if she didn't have anything to give?

Lilli put those thoughts out of her head and started to pack her suitcase. Luke would pick her up and they would head north to Pawley's Island. The only thing that Lilli really knew about Pawley's Island, was that it was famous for expensive hammocks. She looked forward to experiencing the island with Luke. Luke picked Lilli up around 2 p.m. and they headed for the Sea View Inn. As they inched closer to the Inn, Lilli started to get nervous and Luke picked up on this immediately. He told her they were doing the right thing, and everything would be fine and not to worry.

She started to chat a little faster and read off some facts she found on the computer about the Inn. "On one side is a private beach and a pristine salt marsh on the other. The Inn is smack dab in the middle of the island and offers you three meals a day and a perfect beach. Do you like to walk around and experience things on foot?"

"Sure," he said.

"I always loved to take all our visitors on the walking house tour through Summerville. Each time I took the tour, I seemed to discover something new and interesting."

Luke assured her they would explore the island inch by inch and leave no grain of sand unturned. Lilli started to relax, and then before she knew it, they were pulling into the back lot of the Inn.

Chapter 21

The island seemed deserted. There were a few people walking around, but you could count them on one hand. Lilli and Luke got their overnight bags out of the trunk and Luke carried them up one flight of steps to the back door of the Inn. When they stepped inside, it was everything Lilli hoped it would be. It was plain, but charming. You could see the beach and how the ocean met the sand through the many windows in the lobby. A very nice gentleman greeted them and told them that they didn't have too many guests this time of year and he was happy they decided to come. Lilli told him they were looking forward to exploring the island and any suggestions from him would be appreciated. He told them to put on their walking shoes and head down the beach and they would surely see the beauty that Pawley's Island possesses. Once they got to their room, Luke suggested that since they had a few hours before dinner, maybe they could explore the beach. Lilli and Luke held hands and giggled like two teens as they walked, but then Lilli said she should have brought her jacket along on the walk. She was getting a little cold. Luke tucked her closer under his arm and they headed back to the Inn.

As they entered the lobby the young man behind the desk, Harrison, introduced himself and informed them that dinner would be served in less than an hour. They said they were famished and would be there on time. As they went back into the room, the wine and roses that Lilli ordered was now on the coffee table by the fire-place. Lilli loved flowers, especially yellow roses and told Luke that she arranged for them to be sent to the room. Lilli knew Luke wouldn't drink but she asked him to pour her a glass of wine. She just wanted to loosen up a little bit. They sat by the fireplace that Luke had now set ablaze. Cozily, Lilli sipped her wine.

"You look beautiful by fire light," Luke whispered in her ear.

She could feel her cheeks flush and she didn't know if it was from the wine or Luke's light touch. Lilli never could accept a compliment without getting embarrassed.

"Thank you," she said, "you don't look half bad yourself." She leaned into Luke and they kissed.

"You taste delicious," Luke said.

Lilli said, "I haven't heard that saying about kisses being delicious since my cousin Laura told me that years ago." She continued with her story, "My eighty-five-year-old cousin, Laura, fell in love with a much younger man, sixty-year-old Becca. He was her limo driver. The whole family was sure he was just after her money. Maybe he was, but so what. She had plenty. He made her smile. He gave her a reason to live. He called her every day and took her out for lunch a few days a week. He freed her from the home her daughters put her in. He told her she was lovely. He made her feel special when everyone else abandoned her. Her two daughters and twelve grandchildren never kept in touch with her. They only wanted her money and we all knew it. I saw the glow in her eyes when she talked about him. I was the only one to tell her that if he made her happy, she should just go with it. Everyone was mad at me especially when she bought him a black jaguar. She raved about the beautiful car. When she told me that his kisses were delicious, I just knew even if the relationship was one sided, she needed this. When her daughters threatened to have him arrested, that put an end to the relationship, he never came by again. She died alone in that fancy old age home three months later. I know she missed him terribly and died of a broken heart."

They kissed and talked, and the hour passed quickly, so they headed down to the dining room. The dining room was surrounded by large windows, and it was so relaxing listening to the waves crash on the shore. Luke ordered a glass of wine for Lilli. He then ordered a tonic water for himself.

He said, "I would love to order a drink to celebrate our first night together, but because of the flashbacks I've had lately, I know I could never drink again." He told Lilli that he had a flashback just last night, that he woke up and remembered getting thrown out of a bar because of an argument he had over the Steelers of all things. He couldn't remember the bar or town, but lately, bits and pieces were coming back to him about things that happened to him three and four years ago.

Lilli asked, "Are these memories good or bad things to have? Do you want to remember your past?"

Luke said he didn't mind remembering the past, he just hoped there was nothing in the past for him to regret.

Lilli said, "One gains courage by stopping and looking fear in the face. If you can live through the horrors, you can certainly take the next thing that comes along in this life of ours." Lilli assured him that he was a good person and she was sure his indiscretions were all minor.

"I hope and pray you're right," Luke said.

Lilli smiled, "I know I am, I could never love you the way I do if you had a dark evil side."

Luke raised his eyebrows and a half grin and immediately said, "I'm starved, let's order!"

Dinner was great. They both ordered low country boil and devoured it. Since there was nothing to do on the island at night, they decided to sit by the fire in their room. They talked for a few minutes when Luke leaned into Lilli and grabbed her and kissed her like Elgin never did. The kissing didn't stop for a long time and then Luke guided Lilli to the bed.

It was a beautiful four-poster bed with shear curtains draped down its side. The down comforter was tossed aside and then Luke placed Lilli on top of a mountain of soft pillows. She could feel his hard-muscular body against hers. Lilli and Luke undressed at the same time while looking into each other's eyes. Before she knew it, she was making hot uncontrollable love to a man like she never did. Her legs were wrapped around him to bring him even closer into her. As he thrust himself slowly, but forcibly into her he gently placed his tongue on hers, and with each passing motion she was aroused with a passion she had never known. While all this was new to her, it felt so right. She couldn't get enough of

Luke and it seemed he felt the same way. They made love twice and after two hours of being joined as one, Luke suggested they sit by the fire. Luke pulled the down comforter that was already on the floor closer to the fireplace. They snuggled close and then he started kissing her again. This time he caressed her breasts then they laid down on the floor with her on top of him. This was something that rarely happened with Elgin. She just wanted it this way now. She placed Luke inside her and gently moved effortlessly up and down until he came inside her with a loud moan. After they made love, they fell asleep exhausted.

The next morning, Lilli was almost embarrassed at the thought of the way she behaved in bed and then on the floor with Luke. She looked at Luke and he smiled at her and she knew this feeling of being alive once again couldn't be wrong. Luke brought out the life in her that she had given up when Elgin died on Hilltop Road. How could she ever repay him for helping her come back from the darkest place she had ever been.

Lilli tried not to compare Elgin and Luke, but she just couldn't help it. Elgin was her gentle, soft-spoken southern gentleman, a pillar of the community in which she grew up and till this day lived in. Then there was this new man in her life, Luke, who was a wanderer, a little bit aloof and very mysterious. He had no roots and ties to anyone or anything. How could she be attracted to this type of man? Lilli kept analyzing the two men and looked deep for a common thread. She knew there had to be something that connected Elgin and Luke to her. It struck her later that the one thing they both had in common was that they both made her feel safe. She needed that from a man and would be satisfied with that connection for now.

After breakfast, while walking on the beach, Luke asked Lilli if he disturbed her sleep last night. Lilli said she didn't hear a thing, "Were you okay? Were you sick?"

They sat down on the deserted beach. Luke said he had another flashback and this time it was different from any other. "Tell me about it and maybe I can help you decipher it?"

He laughed and said he didn't think so, but he told her about the flashing lights. Lilli tried to pin him down on the type of lights. He only remembered they were red, white and flashing furiously. Lilli told him not to push and his memory would come back to him eventually. He said he thought he remembered looking out his car window and seeing a woman standing there.

She could see how confused and utterly frustrated Luke was getting so she told him, "Put it out of your mind for today." They kissed and headed back to explore the salt marsh on the opposite side of the island. As they stood out on the long docks, they were fascinated at the egrets and how they stood so still on one leg while keeping an eye out for their next meal. Luke and Lilli talked for the longest time. The world with its wonderful and amazing creatures of nature never looked so beautiful.

After a light lunch, they decided to take a car ride to the end of the island. They both agreed that Pawley's Island was a great place to visit, but they could never live there for any length of time. They returned from their brief car ride and went to their room. They lit the fire and Lilli asked, "Do you think three o'clock is too early for a glass of wine?" This was all so new to her that she felt a glass of wine could only help relax her before the love making started.

Luke assured her it wasn't too early and filled her glass. As she sipped her wine and watched the fire do a dance for her, she thought that life couldn't be better. When she finished her wine, Lilli and Luke went over to the bed and once again made love excitedly and almost as furiously as the crackling of the fire.

Before this weekend, she thought she was too old, but then she once again let out with groans so deep from inside her they almost sounded like they were coming from another person. This couldn't be her. She melted into his arms and they fell asleep together, her on top. Luke started to move around a lot and woke Lilli. She gently got off him and she went to the bathroom for a drink of water. When she returned, she could see Luke thrashing around the bed and she woke him up. She told him he looked like he was having a nightmare.

Luke grabbed her and kissed her hard, then he brought Lilli into him and before they knew it they were making love once more. This time it seemed to be out of necessity instead of passion. Luke was holding on so tightly that Lilli had to ask him to ease up on his grip a little. Luke told her he never wanted to let go of her. "I finally found the one thing that was always missing in my life and now I'm scared to death of losing it."

Lilli looked at him and softly said, "Luke, I love you and will stick by you through good times and bad, I won't give up on us, so don't worry about losing me."

Luke smiled, and Lilli kissed him gently. For a long time, they lay there quietly and peacefully in each other's arms. The rest of the day flew by, and when they left the island, they knew this was something special. They knew it was right.

Chapter 22

Luke took Lilli to her front door and kissed her goodbye. He told her he'd call her later. Lilli listened to the eight calls that were flashing on her voicemail. She called her daughters to tell them that she arrived home. All the girls were polite and asked if she had a good time. Lilli told them it was delightful, and by the lilt in her voice, it was hard not to believe her. Lilli then called Phyllis and told her what a wonderful time she had with Luke on Pawley's Island. Phyllis was genuinely happy for her. She started to ask her questions, then Lilli made plans with her to have breakfast the next morning. There was a call from Savannah Grace, which Lilli put off returning until later that evening. She was hoping Savannah was out to dinner and could just leave a message. No such luck, Savannah answered the phone and Lilli was put on the hot seat.

"How was your weekend with Luke? Was the sex everything you thought it would be? What did you talk about, a future together?" Savannah Grace beckoned anxiously, yet sarcastically.

She answered all her questions without giving away too much. Lilli told her that they had a wonderful time and he's as wonderful as she had imagined. She knew that Carolyn, JoAnn and the rest of the tennis gang would be filled in on her weekend with Luke before the night was over. Lilli hung up the phone and smiled. She was so happy and no one or nothing could ruin her high spirits right now.

She started to walk around the house and open curtains, shutters, and lights. Her beautiful two-story Victorian that stood so tall and was filled with happiness for so many years had seemed to come to life again. She went into the living room and sat down on the sofa. She sat in Elgin's favorite spot and gazed around the room. It was such a warm home decorated with pictures of their life together. On the mantel, she looked at the six Lladro statues of little girls and boys. Every time a new grandchild came into their lives, Elgin bought her a statue for them. She looked up the hallway stairs and could see all the pictures of her family. For so many months she hadn't noticed them at all while walking in the dark to her bedroom. As she walked upstairs to unpack, she gazed out into the garden. The yellow roses that Elgin planted for her were still blooming. The two weeping cherry trees in honor of her parents who passed away so suddenly tilted toward each other and it made her smile. How did she miss all this beauty for so long? She realized that Luke was the one that brought the beauty of life and love back into her heart.

The phone rang, it was Luke. He asked her if she was hungry and she said, "Starved." He told her he would be over in an hour and they would head on out of town to Mario's for a late dinner.

Lilli asked him if they could just go to the diner in town since she was a little tired. "I would give my right arm for a greasy burger from the Blue Bay Diner." Luke said that sounded good to him also.

Once Luke got to Lilli's house, he admitted that he laid down for a few minutes after unpacking and fell asleep until another disturbing dream woke him up. Luke told her that someone was screaming for help and crying hysterically in his dream. Luke said he wanted to get out of his car and help her, but he couldn't get the door opened. He confessed that when he woke up, he was sweating and shaking like a child coming out of a night terror.

Lilli grew silent for a minute and thought. What could she say to help…nothing?

Lilli told him that she would call Linda Richardson, her grief counselor, tomorrow morning and find out the name of the best doctor to help him try to get to the bottom of these horrible nightmares. He said the flashbacks were coming nightly as of late and he had to find out if they were real or fantasy. He suggested to Lilli that maybe he needed a doctor that could hypnotize him. Lilli assured him that Linda would steer him in the right direction, and even if they had to drive to a larger city like Charleston or Charlotte they would.

At the Blue Bay Diner, as Lilli enjoyed her thick medium rare cheeseburger, she told Luke that she was thinking of getting her Jaguar out of the garage and back on the road. She was ready to move forward even further, and this would be the next step for her. Luke smiled and said that was great. Lilli then asked Luke to come home with her and uncover the car that had been entombed in her garage for the last few years. Her son-in-law had disconnected the battery and then every few months would connect it and make sure that it started up. Lilli continued the insurance and property tax payments since Elgin had died. He loved that car and she just knew she could never part with it.

After dinner, they returned to the house and gently lifted the cover off the silver jaguar that sat in her garage since that fateful rainy night Elgin left her. Elgin's smell had long left the car but sitting in it made her smile when she thought of him. Luke reconnected the battery and said the car was in great shape and she should drive it every day. As Lilli heard the car start up the blood from her face drained. Luke noticed this immediately and asked her if she wanted to go for a drive. Lilli knew she had to take this step, so she got behind the wheel for the first time in over two years. Luke told her he was proud of her and assured her it would get easier each day. Lilli just smiled and held the wheel tightly as she backed out of the garage.

Luke whispered once again, "I love you so much, Lilli."

Chapter 23

As Lilli had promised, the next morning she called Linda Richardson and got the name of a doctor in Charlotte who specialized in cases that sounded like Luke's. Her specialty is repressed memories due to trauma. Lilli called Luke immediately after hanging up and told him to get ready for a road trip to Charlotte. She told him that as soon as she could secure an appointment, she would be taking him to see Dr. Patricia Panicco. Luke gave Lilli his schedule for the next few weeks and then she made the call. Lilli got an appointment for the following Monday afternoon. Luke was pleased and said that it couldn't come soon enough.

Next, Lilli had a wonderful breakfast with her cousin Phyllis. She told Phyllis that she had the best time with Luke. She never would have imagined anyone could fill her days or nights ever again, but Luke does. She wants Phyllis to meet him soon. Phyllis told her, "I like him already Lilli. I see the glow he has put back on your face and that's enough for me. After Elgin died my heart broke whenever I looked at the sadness in your eyes."

Lilli and Luke saw each other regularly now and had sex often, but always in Luke's apartment. Never could she be with him in Elgin's bed. Lilli knew it was silly, but she still felt uncomfortable just kissing Luke goodnight in the front hallway of her house. Everywhere she looked in her house she saw Elgin.

Monday morning, Lilli and Luke started out for Charlotte. They had the directions programmed into the navigational system, and after a quick stop at the Bagel Bin for coffee and an egg bagel they were off. Little did they know where this road to Charlotte would really lead them.

Luke seemed very nervous and Lilli reassured him that there was probably nothing in his past that he was hiding, "It will be good that we finally find out what has you so upset." She continued, "No matter what it is, we can and will handle it together."

The ride to Charlotte was uneventful as the directions led them right to the middle of the city and to the office building of Dr. Pat Panicco, on Trade Street. As they walked hand in hand to the elevator, Lilli could feel Luke's hand sweating.

She leaned up and kissed his cheek so softly and whispered to him, "I will be there for you and help you through whatever comes our way today and always."

Luke smiled and told her, "I hope today is my first step out of this black hole I seem to have fallen into. What scares me to death is that you won't be there once I come out the other side."

Lilli told him again that she would help him through this and never leave him no matter what happens. They opened the door to Dr. Panicco's office and found only one person waiting quietly. The receptionist asked for his name and made Luke fill out the insurance papers and lots of personal information.

Luke signed his name and handed the papers back to the

receptionist. Someone then exited the inner office and the lady waiting got up to meet the gentlemen and asked him how it went today. He said fine and then they made an appointment for next week and left without a word spoken. Luke hoped that he wouldn't have to come back week after week.

Lilli said, "Whatever it takes, we will do." The next ten minutes seemed to drag by and finally, Nina, the receptionist, came over to Luke and told him to follow her to the doctor's office. Luke got up and looked at Lilli with such fear that it made her heart sink a little.

Lilli made the hour go a little quicker by reading magazines and recipes. She even pulled two recipes out of a magazine and tucked them into her purse. When the doctor's door opened, Luke emerged looking a little pale. Lilli hoped this meant that he had a break through. Luke scheduled another appointment, got a prescription for Xanax and they left. As soon as the office door closed behind him, Lilli asked him what happened.

Luke said, "I think the session went well and I really liked Dr. Pat, but no breakthrough yet. Dr. Pat assured me that they would find out what was causing me such distress, but it might take a while. She said she'd first like to try some talking sessions and then work up to drugs to force me back in time if necessary. I just want the nightmares to stop."

Lilli told him to hold on a little longer and they would come to an end soon. Luke seemed a little optimistic, but deep down he was a little disappointed because he wanted this torture over today. He didn't want to wait another day to be free of his torment.

Dr. Pat's schedule was pretty booked for the next month, but she gave him some pills to take the edge off his nightmares. On the ride back to Summerville, Luke was relatively quiet. Lilli could feel his anxiety and tried to talk about the simple pleasures in life and the fact that she was so happy since he came into her life. Luke shuffled and tried to smile, but still couldn't shake this feeling of nearing disaster. Lilli asked him to go away for the weekend with her, but he had to work. Secretly, Luke was relieved because he didn't want to have Lilli hear or see him toss and turn in his tormented sleep.

Luke told Lilli he was tired and just wanted to get his prescription filled and go to bed early. He even wanted to skip dinner. Lilli advised him that he should eat a little something before he takes his Xanax. He agreed and after a quick bite, he dropped her home.

Once he got home, he laid down on the couch and Snickers jumped right up on his chest. He took a Xanax after an hour because he just couldn't settle himself. As he stroked his kitten's back, he closed his eyes, but every time he did, he would see red lights. He thought he was going crazy but finally drifted off to sleep. As he slept, he saw Lilli. Where was she? Where was he? Why couldn't he fill in the gaps? Luke woke up with a jolt and decided to take another Xanax. He also thought about his addictive personality, but he needed to sleep. He needed to forget. Finally, sleep came and it was dreamless at last.

Chapter 24

When Lilli got home, she went in the kitchen to feed Gigi. Then she went into the dining room and sat at the long farm table and thought back to the many family dinners she served there to her family. She remembered one particular night before the presidential election. The political discussions with her sons-in-law had gotten a little heated. The Jackson Clan were staunch republicans from way back and now they had to let some young democrats eat at their table.

Elgin would say, "Lilli, I must be getting old if I can sit here patiently and listen to these boys and their slanted political views without thinking about getting my rifle." The girls would all laugh.

"It's a new world Daddy," Tammy would say, "listen to Dana, he has some valid points to make."

Elgin would tell Lilli, "I can't listen to them on an empty stomach, please let's eat."

They would all laugh and get dinner on the table. Yes, it was a happy house. It was a house filled with smiles and love. No one would have ever dreamed that it would be the last election Elgin would ever participate in.

After a long while she went upstairs and undressed. She saw the pretty little flowered box sitting on her dresser. The box of love letters from Elgin. She hadn't looked at them in a long time. She read the last one Elgin had written to her for her birthday:

To my one true love. I am so lucky to be loving you each and every day. I pray that we can be together for many years to come. I hope as we grow old, I will never lose my memory because then I would lose the thoughts of the best years of my life that was spent with you, my darling.

Lilli smiled and laid down on the bed. It would be a quiet evening since Luke was going to stay home anyway. She started to doze but didn't want to fall asleep so early, and as she went into her closet to put some clothes away, she was surrounded by Elgin's suits, shoes, shirts, and the many ties he had worn to court over the years. She knew she should start thinking about giving his clothes to their church clothing drive soon. Her heart just wasn't ready to do it. She thought of Elgin and their many years together.

She smiled and said aloud, "I still love you Elgin, I will always love you and never forget you."

As she shut the light in the closet the light bulb blew out. Was that a sign from Elgin? Her daughter Noelle firmly believed that light bulbs blowing out were signs from your dead loved ones telling you that they are there with you. She felt like she needed a sign from Elgin. She hoped Noelle was right. She fell asleep with thoughts of Elgin. Still hoping he knew she wasn't being unfaithful to him. She would always love him.

It was early the next morning when the phone rang. Lilli jumped because most of her friends and family never called before 9 a.m.

"Hello darling Lilli," Luke's voice was so happy. "I know I'm breaking the nine o'clock rule, but I just had to talk to you."

"What is it Luke, you sound so happy?"

Luke rambled on about how great he slept and how refreshed he feels. "I can't wait to see you today." Lilli admitted she was anxious to see him, too. Luke asked, "Are you nervous about coming to the club and seeing all your friends?"

Lilli replied, "I love you, Luke, and I don't care who knows it."

Lilli got to the club early and ran into Steve. Steve said, "You look wonderful Lilli. So, I guess it's true what I've been hearing about you and Luke."

Lilli would never lie to Steve, so she told him how it started with Luke and how she slowly fell in love with him. Steve told her that he was happy for her and jealous of Luke. Lilli looked shocked as Steve continued, "You must have known that I was waiting in the wings till you were ready to move on with your life Lilli."

She said quietly, "No, Steve I never knew. I'm sorry. You know I love you, but not that way."

He smiled a tough smile, the kind of smile that is forced when pain is abruptly present, and said, "I'm happy you are moving on with your life again Lilli. I hated to see you so sad. I was hoping that someday you would move on with me." Chagrined, he put his head down and walked away.

Lilli continued downstairs to the locker room. She checked the sign-in sheet for the double's tennis group today. Oh no, she was playing with the biggest club gossips, Donna and Angela. They would pump her and find out everything then pass it around the clubhouse by nightfall. It's funny because Lilli didn't even care. She was in love and that was all there was to it.

Lilli could sense the younger staff members glaring at her. She just remembered her favorite line from *Gone with The Wind*, "pea green with envy." It made her half smile as she passed by them. All the younger girls were trying to snag Luke. She was a little surprised when she heard Kimberly, the club manager, telling Judy and Julie that the only reason Luke went with her was because she was loaded.

Kimberly had the nerve to say, "He could now retire and live in style with his sugar momma."

Luke left the locker room and ran into Lilli on her way to the court.

She told him what she just heard, and he asked, "Do you think that is the reason?" She shook her head no. He continued, "I love you and if all I wanted was money all I had to do was go back to Pittsburgh and take over my Dad's business." Again, he put her doubts to rest.

Lilli saw all her friends staring at her and said, "Hi ladies, are we going to play tennis or not?"

Everyone took their positions. Lilli spoke up and said, "I'll be glad to answer all your questions at lunch today. We've been friends for too long to start whispering behind each other's backs."

Everyone agreed, and Irene jokingly said, "Let's get on with this match so we can go to lunch." Everyone laughed, especially Lilli.

Tennis went by quicker than usual and they gathered for lunch in the dining room. Irene started the conversation, "Lilli, we are all happy that you are smiling again, but you must realize that this came as a complete shock to us all."

Lilli grinned, "It was more of a shock to me I can assure you girls." Lilli got serious, "After Elgin died, I didn't think I could ever move on. I would lay in bed each night after I splashed his Old Spice cologne on my wrist. I would smell my wrist until my Ambien put me to sleep. Then I would wake up a few hours later and cry myself back to sleep each night. After two very long, and sad years I found myself able to live again and then shockingly love again. Something I never thought would happen to me, but it did. I know Elgin would want me to love again and I hope my friends do, too."

"Of course, we do, Lilli." Savannah Grace put her arm around Lilli, "If you are happy with Luke, please know that I will stand by you. Also know, that if he hurts you dear friend, I'm going after him with both barrels loaded and ready to shoot." Everyone was hysterical because they knew Savannah meant it.

The afternoon went smoother than Lilli expected. It was fun. Some of the girls got a little too personal and Lilli just said, "That's a bit much, next question." They all wanted to know about his background. Lilli filled them in on his family, schooling, and travels across the country. They all said he was hot. Lilli agreed.

Now that all of Lilli's friends had come to grips with the idea of her and Luke, it was finally time for Luke to meet her daughters.

Chapter 25

Lilli called her girls and told them to secure babysitters for Sunday night and to meet her and Luke at Mario's Restaurant. Carlton was the only one who had ever heard of the tiny little house way out on the edge of town.

Lilli knew that there could be no better place than Mario's to share Luke with them. That is the place that he shared himself with her. Luke and Lilli were the first to arrive. The girls and their husbands came in one car. Lilli could only imagine the conversations on the half hour drive to the restaurant.

Noelle bounded in first, followed by Jeanne and Tammy who brought up the rear. The restaurant was empty since it was so early. They had no problem seeing Lilli and Luke sitting at a table set for eight. They all said a polite hello and then commented on how surprised they were to find this wonderful little restaurant in the middle of nowhere.

Mario and Gia came over to the table and Lilli proudly introduced her family to them. Then as soon as the introductions were over, the feast began. First, the bruschetta arrived followed by the garlic bread with mozzarella cheese melted on top.

Luke told them, "I have taken the liberty of leaving our food choices to Mario. He will bring out the most delicious array of

Italian food that you have ever tasted." They all said it sounded good to them.

Of course, Noelle asked about the wine choices. Luke told her that Lilli always drank the house Chianti and loved it.

Carlton said, "I love Chianti, I will go with that, too."

Noelle, the family wine snob, agreed Chianti was the way to go with Italian food. Anthony appeared with seven wine goblets. He knew that Luke wouldn't drink so he skipped him when placing the wine glasses down on the table. Then Mario brought over two large straw wrapped bottles of Chianti. He poured a healthy amount in each of the seven glasses. Everyone picked up their glasses when Lilli made a quick toast to "new beginnings."

Tammy turned to Luke, "Aren't you drinking?"

Luke replied, "I don't drink anymore, it doesn't agree with me."

She looked at him suspiciously. She stored this in back of her mind in order to ask her Mom later if he was an alcoholic. Next, the hot stuffed pepper and fried calamari arrived. The girls didn't touch these two items, but Lilli and the men did. The feast contin-ued, gnocchi's, chicken and shrimp parmigiana. The side dishes were just as wonderful, escarole sautéed in garlic oil and zucchini flowers. These flowers came from the zucchini plant and were dipped in a flour and water mixture then deep-fried. The whole ta-ble agreed that the zucchini flowers were amazing. They couldn't believe they were actually eating flowers.

Lilli was eating everything that was brought to the table and her girls commented on how her palate had grown. She smiled at them, "Mario and Gia have insisted I try all the traditional dishes and I have grown to love most of them. The tentacles of the calamari are still a no-go for me though."

Her sons-in-law laughed, but she noticed her daughters only smiled cautiously. Getting accustomed to their new Mom was taking them a little longer than Lilli would like.

Noelle had now downed three large glasses of Chianti and was letting loose with the questions they all had for Luke. She wanted to know why he didn't live in Pittsburgh, why he chose Summerville, why he had no ex-wife at his age or children.

The questions continued until Lilli turned to Luke and said, "By now you probably have guessed that Noelle was a journalism major in college."

Noelle continued, "You have to ask to find out the who, what, where, when, and why was our motto in school." They all laughed, including Luke.

Last, but certainly not least, a tray of Italian desserts was brought to the table. They all tried the Italian cheesecake made with ricotta, the cannoli, zeppole, and the cake the restaurant called Mario's cake. Their favorite by far was Mario's cake. A two-layer delicate white cake with delicious Italian styled cream in the middle. Then Anthony brought over a tray with eight small demitasse cups filled with espresso. Mario and Gia followed with the Sambuca and coffee beans. Gia placed three beans in all the cups as Mario poured the Sambuca very generously. He knew to skip Luke's cup. Lilli asked if any of the girls knew the significance of the three coffee beans. They didn't, so she explained the Italian custom.

Jeanne looked at Lilli, "I can't believe how proficient you have become in the Italian culture."

Tammy looked at Luke, "Are you Italian, Luke?"

He said he wasn't, but said Mario and Gia taught him all about their traditions, food, and culture over the past few years. By the tone of Tammy's voice, it was obvious that Lilli would have to convince her the most that she deserved a second chance in life with Luke. Lilli realized that because she was Elgin's baby and he coddled her the most, it would be most difficult for her to accept this new love with Luke.

Noelle was the only one who enjoyed the espresso and Sambuca. She said it tasted like licorice. The night was coming to an end and all the small talk was over. Everyone had just spent three hours scrutinizing Luke and interacting with him and their mother as a couple. It hurt to see their Mom with anyone but their Dad, but the girls decided not to tell her that. She did look very happy. All her sons-in-law wanted to pay the bill, but Luke said it was his pleasure to buy them all dinner.

The goodbyes were all said and as Lilli watched her daughters get into Carlton's Denali, she said, "I'd love to be a fly on the windshield in that car tonight."

Luke looked at her and they both laughed.

On the ride home, the girls took their positions.

Noelle stated, "At least he's handsome and not some shriveled up old man."

Carlton shook his head and smiled.

Tammy divulged, "I don't trust him, I think he's only after our Moms' money. I've seen lots of programs on cat-fishing of older lonely women."

Dana interjected, "Dear, you have to give him a chance. You can't deny your Mom looks very happy. You don't want her to be alone, forever, do you?"

Jamie said, "Well, I like him. He seems like a down to earth guy and being from Pittsburgh, that makes him extra nice!"

They all laughed.

Jeanne said she was still worried how Gabby and Nicky would feel about Luke. "They were so attached to Dad, and now to see this man with Mom might be too much."

Jamie remarked, "The kids will all adapt better than you three." Carlton and Dana agreed.

Tammy confessed her uneasiness, "I shiver at the thought of Mom having sex with Luke. The visual is just too disturbing!"

And with that, the rest of the ride was filled with chatter about absolutely nothing important.

Chapter 26

Weeks quickly turned into months and Luke continued to see Dr. Pat. After no substantial breakthrough, she decided to try drugs to bring Luke back to face his fears.

Dr. Pat told Luke, "You can't solve your problem Luke, without first knowing the problem."

Lilli and Luke arrived early for his appointment as they did for all the previous ones. They could have made this frequent journey to Charlotte with their eyes closed by now.

Luke looked at Lilli, "I hope you are still here waiting for me once I find out the truth that is buried so far down inside me. The truth that is haunting me and the one that I am obviously trying to hide so desperately."

Lilli squeezed his hand gently, "I will be here waiting for you when you come out Luke. I don't really think there is any deep dark horrible secret inside you, but if there is, we will face it together. You are a good man, I just know it. I can feel it in my heart."

Luke's face was white with fear, "God, Lilli, I love you so much. I don't want to lose you."

Lilli leaned into him and kissed him on his cheek and whispered in his ear, "You will never lose me, Luke."

With that said, the door opened and they saw Dr. Pat standing there. "Are you ready to try and get to the bottom of this today Luke?" she inquired. He just nodded and followed her into her office like a frightened child.

She laid Luke down on a recliner and administered an IV and almost instantly he was somewhere else in time. Then he heard Dr. Pat's voice from a far-off place.

"Luke, can you hear me?"

Luke replied in a very weak voice, "Yes."

"Luke, I want to take you back to that rainy night and the flashing lights you keep talking about, can I do that?"

Barely audible now, "Yes."

"Luke can you speak up?" she said.

He raised his voice a tad louder and said, "OK."

She continued questioning him, "Where are you Luke? Can you see a sign on the road?"

He squeezed his eyes shut tighter and whispered, "It's so dark and wet."

"Where is the road Luke?"

He replied, "I don't know."

"Look for a street sign, Luke."

He said, "It's too dark, I can't see one."

She pressed on, "Why are you on this road?"

His body was twitching and thrashing about uncontrollably now, "I'm going back to Pittsburgh." He then shrieked, "Oh no, I can't stop, I'm skidding off the road. I don't want to..."

Dr. Pat didn't want to press him anymore. She knew they had a great breakthrough today, but realized going further in his condition might harm him more than help him today. She removed the IV from his arm and brought him back. When Luke came around, she told him they had made a lot of progress, but she didn't want to press him anymore because he became agitated and didn't want to add to his anxiety. She then told him everything he had said, and you could see he was shaken to his core. He had a million questions, but no answers.

"Did I hurt someone?"

"I don't have that answer for you yet, Luke, but come back next week and we'll pick up where we left off and find out what's buried deep inside you. We will find out what is making you so sad. What you are so afraid of."

Luke walked out to the waiting room and Lilli could see that he was quite upset.

Lilli had heard him yell out from the closed office door. She was sitting on the edge of her chair. Luke made an appointment for the very next week, at the same time. Lilli and Luke walked hand in hand to the elevator.

"Did you make a breakthrough, Luke? I heard you yell out something."

"Yes," he said shyly, shaking his head.

"Tell me everything, Luke."

"Lilli, I saw the road. Then I remember saying I didn't want to hurt anyone."

Lilli gasped, "Hurt who, Luke?"

Luke replied, "I don't know, but I guess I will find that out next week."

Lilli's mind was now racing in all directions now. Her main question was when did Luke come to Summerville? She didn't meet him at the club till the spring. They said he just moved in to Summerville in early spring.

Luke dropped Lilli home and she knew she had to tell someone, but whom could she trust? Her suspicions were all over the board now. She would talk to her cousin Phyllis. When she didn't answer the phone, she called her other cousin Lorraine, to see if her sister Phyllis was there visiting her. Lorraine said Phyllis just left her house with Momma Lena and should be home in a little while.

Lorraine asked if she was alright, and could she help, "You sound upset Lilli, is something wrong?"

She told Lorraine she just wanted to chit chat it was no big deal. Lilli hung up feeling anxious and nauseous. She waited an hour and called Phyllis.

Phyllis told her, "Don't speculate, you're probably torturing your-self for nothing. Let the doctor get to the bottom of it next week and then you can figure things out. I'm sure it's nothing."

They hung up and Lilli puttered around, walking in circles and doing absolutely nothing for the next few hours. She then made a little plate of food and went upstairs early and watched the news.

She tossed and turned for most of the night and when the first light came through the shutters, she closed her eyes and finally got a few hours rest.

Chapter 27

The week was dragging at a snail's pace for Lilli and Luke. They were both gripped deep with impending fear. There was nothing either one of them could do or say to lift this black cloud from them.

They didn't see each other much that week, but talked daily. They never talked about Dr. Pat or her revelations last week. Phyllis was right, what good would it do to speculate. Luke kept making excuses about working more and she accepted them freely. They were both getting themselves ready for the worst possible news.

Lilli was bringing herself back to Elgin's death daily. She thought about Luke's timeline in coming to Summerville nonstop. It was all a haze to her because of Elgin's passing. Those days turned into months. She couldn't sort it out in her mind. She wouldn't let her mind take her there. It couldn't be.

Sunday night was spent at Mario's for a lovely dinner. Gia and Mario sat with Luke and Lilli for a little while, but could tell they were different tonight, but wouldn't pry.

"Why don't you two have some espresso, with Sambuca?" Gia encouraged, "It will perk you both up."

Lilli accepted, but Luke refused.

As Lilli sipped her espresso with Sambuca, Luke apologized to her. "I'm sorry for being such a mess this past week Lilli, but I'm scared to death of what tomorrow may bring. I know both of us are thinking the same thing but too afraid to say it out loud. If we say it out loud then it may be real."

"Luke, don't say another word," Lilli said softly. "It is probably going to turn out to be nothing."

He conjectured, "We both know deep in our hearts that it is something and something bad."

Luke paid the bill and the half hour ride back to Summerville was eerily quiet.

When they got to Lilli's house, Luke walked her to the front door. She asked Luke if he wanted to come in.

Luke replied, "I'm the worst company you could have right now. I just want to go to sleep with the help of my Xanax and get myself ready for our last trek to Charlotte."

Lilli kissed him gently and said, "I'm sure after your session with Dr. Pat tomorrow, you will find that there is nothing to dread. This will all be put to rest. I love you, Luke."

He said he loved her too and hugged her for a long time. He started to walk away and turned and gave her a half smile and waved. He felt very alone at this point, just like when his mother died. Ever since he met Lilli, he never allowed himself back to that lonely place. Why was he brought back there now?

Chapter 28

They arrived at the doctor's office an hour early this time. Luke fidgeted, and Lilli tried in vain to calm him down.

Lilli, still trying to comfort him said, "In a couple of hours, we will put this behind us and you will be able to sleep once more in peace. We will be able to move on with our lives."

He looked at her and gave a sheepish grin.

Finally, Dr. Pat stuck her head out of the office and said, "Be with you in a minute, Luke."

His hands started to sweat, and the color drained out of his face once again. Fear had him in its grips and there was nothing any-one could say, or do, to change that now.

A short time later the office door opened, and Luke got up and walked slowly toward Dr. Pat and his past. Again, she laid him down on her recliner and administered the IV.

Dr. Pat waited a few minutes, "Luke let's go back to that dark night on that wet road. What road is it? Look for a sign. Do you see any people on the road? Can you see any faces?"

Luke whispered, "Yes."

The questioning continued, "Who is it, is it a man or a woman?"

"He's leaning into the window of a car parked on the side of the road."

Suddenly, Luke bolted straight up and yelled at the top of his lungs, "Be careful, get out of the way, step back, you're going to get hit! Oh my God, don't hit him! Step on the brake!"

Dr. Pat drilled him with more questions. She wanted to end this mystery today, right now…end it once and for all so they could all move on with their lives. The last few questions that would put this all to rest were now upon Luke.

"Who has to step on the brake Luke, is it you?"

Tears were streaming down Luke's face in a gush. "Yes, I have to step harder on the brake. I'm going to hit him, too. Oh, dear Jesus, he's flying into the air. It's so dark, I can't see anyone. Oh God, what just happened? I hope this is a dream."

She lowered her tone, "Luke, you said you didn't want to hit him, too. Tell me what you meant. Did someone else hit him?"

Luke stammered over the next few sentences.

With confusion and fear he said, "There's, there's a woman. She's running into the road. She's crying and screaming over his body, he's not moving."

Dr. Pat was relentless in her questioning now.

"Luke, did another car hit him or you? Luke, look closer. Did your car hit him?"

Luke, now sobbing, "I'm not sure anymore, I'm scared, I'm drunk, I drove off into the darkness. I called for help, don't know what I told the 911 operator."

Luke's sobs had become uncontrollable.

He gasped, "I, I saw Lilli's face. It was Lilli crying there."

Luke wept.

Dr. Pat knew there was no more to Luke's story now. "Please calm down, Luke. It's over now, I'm going to bring you back."

Luke lay quietly for a good 10 minutes, then sat up with Dr. Pat's help.

"I saw that night happening in slow motion all over again. Could it be Lilli's husband? Lilli will never forgive me for leaving them there alone on that starless, dark rainy night."

Dr. Pat reached out and gently touched the top of Luke's hand, "You called 911 to get them help. You did the best you could at that time in your life. There is still that question as to whether another red car hit Elgin first. Don't give up on you and Lilli just yet. People are more forgiving than you expect. Give her a chance to absorb it all. Maybe she saw the other car."

His face was buried in his hands now as he shook his head in disbelief. "How can I go out there and face her?"

Dr. Panicco said she would bring Lilli back when he was ready to see her. Together they would tell her what just happened. Luke shook his head in agreement.

Chapter 29

Lilli was led back to the office where she found Luke sitting with his head still buried in his hands.

She sat down beside him, "Luke, are you ok? Luke, look at me."

Lilli looked at Dr. Pat for help. Dr. Panicco felt so sorry for Lilli now, as she knew she would have to explain all of this to her.

She started, "Lilli I want you to be calm and listen to the whole story before you react. Luke revealed a lot of disturbing facts in this session. Some will be hard to hear, but then there is a chance that we can go further and maybe come to a different conclusion."

"I don't understand, Luke look at me," Lilli said firmly. "I'm here for you. Tell me what you saw." Luke then stared at Lilli, but the words were stuck deep down as he opened his mouth to speak. Nothing came out as his lips moved.

Lilli looked to Dr. Pat with fear in her eyes. "You have to tell me what just happened."

Just then, Luke spoke ever so softly that Lilli had to move closer to his mouth to hear him, "Lilli, I was there on the night you lost Elgin. I saw it unfold again, I saw you in the rain."

Lilli was in disbelief, "It's impossible, Luke, I would have remembered you."

Dr. Pat stopped Lilli, "Please let him continue."

Lilli froze in her seat and stared at him as he continued, "I was drunk at the time and when I saw Elgin get hit by the car I couldn't stop because I already had a few DUI's against my record. One more DUI and my license would be revoked and I would have to go to jail. I was a coward and took the safest way out for me."

Lilli started to cry, "No, I don't believe it. You are a kind person with a good heart. You wouldn't have hit him and left me there, no matter the consequences."

Lilli gasped.

Luke took her hands, "Lilli, I was in a different place in my life then. I only took care of and cared about me. If I could take it all back I would. How can I make it right? I love you, please forgive me. Don't hate me, I couldn't bare that."

Dr. Pat interjected and said, "Lilli, Luke seems to think there might have been another red car that hit Elgin first. What do you think about that, did you see another car?"

Lilli stood up and walked toward the door. Dr. Pat asked her to come back, but she continued to the outer office as if in a trance.

Lilli looked back to see Luke and Dr. Pat following her and said in a dry tone, "I only saw one red car."

Lilli walked straight to the elevator as Luke followed sheepishly behind.

Silence.

The motor to the elevator droned as they went down further into the silence.

Once in the car, Lilli turned herself toward her door and propped her head on the window. Luke started to talk after about a half hour and Lilli in an almost robot-like voice told him to stop talking. Luke respected her wishes and for the rest of the ride her head was still pressed up against the window. She found her hand over her mouth. She knew if she started talking, she could never take the words back.

Once they reached Summerville, Lilli spoke for the first time, "Please drop me off at the cemetery." As they pulled up to the front gate, Lilli told Luke to go home.

He said, "I can't leave you out here all alone after what we just found out."

She repeated, wincing her eyes, "Please, just go. I will call Steve to pick me up. I need this time alone."

He said he would call her later. She closed the door and didn't respond or look back. Luke left the cemetery, all alone and with a broken heart once more.

Chapter 30

Lilli walked in a daze to Elgin's grave. She fell onto his grave and started to whisper to him and tears followed for the longest time. She stayed with Elgin for over two hours and finally got up and went to the bench nearest his grave. She then started the long walk to the gate.

Along the way she read the saying, "If love could have saved you, you would have lived forever."

"I would have saved you if I could have. I love you, Elgin. I always did and always will. What should I do, Elgin? Should I forgive? Oh, dear sweet Elgin, how is that even possible?"

She called Steve and asked him to come to the cemetery to pick her up.

"Lilli, has your car broken down? Are you ok?" he inquired.

She just asked him again to come to the gate and she would be waiting there. Within the next ten minutes Steve was hugging her. She felt safe in his arms once more just like the night that Elgin died. She knew she could and would count on him now. He seemed to be the one she leaned on when someone she loved died. This was now another death to her. He could see that she was broken. He opened the door of his car and put Lilli in. He knew not to question her. She would confide in him soon enough.

She looked at him and said softly, "I can't talk about it now, but I promise we will talk soon. Just take me home, please."

Steve looked at her lovingly, "Whatever you need from me Lilli, I'll be here for you. Always."

As they drove down Cemetery Hill Road towards Lilli's house, Steve softly spoke, "I'm off for the next few days so reach out to me any time of day or night, anything you need."

Lilli spoke, "There is nothing I need and nothing anyone can do to help me now."

The rest of the ride they sat in silence. As they pulled into the driveway, Steve got out and opened the door for her. He wrapped his arm around her and she leaned on him as he walked her to the front door. He took her key out of her hand and opened her door.

With sadness pouring out of her body now she told him, "Thank you for rescuing me, I will call you soon."

He caressed her face, "I will be waiting to hear from you." And with that, he walked up her driveway and drove away.

Once in the house, she noticed the red flashing light on her phone. She went closer to the phone and saw that there were lots of missed calls. She was sure the bulk of those were from Luke, but she didn't listen to them. She just couldn't hear his voice right now. She had to be alone with her thoughts. She had to sort this all out.

How would she ever be able to explain this to her girls? They would hate him to the depths of their soul for taking their Dad away from them and then taking their mother to bed. She had to lay down.

She walked up to the bedroom she shared with Elgin and was so thankful she never shared this special room with Luke. The man who was her lover was the man who killed her husband.

This was still her pristine and almost sacred private place that she could come to and be with her Elgin once more. She lay down and her eyes were heavy with tears, so she closed them and drifted off to a light sleep.

She started to revisit the night of the accident in her semi-conscious state. This was something she hadn't done in such a long time. She saw the red car throw Elgin onto the wet pavement. She was searching for a second car. No one ever mentioned a second car. The police never said it, the people with the flat tire never said it, and she never saw it.

Talking out loud to herself, "Was there any way I could have missed another car that night? I would have noticed. NO, NO, NO......Luke you did this. You took away my Elgin!"

Lilli thought that Luke said there was another car because he couldn't bring himself to face the truth in his own drunken stupor. He had convinced himself and skewed the facts, so he could move on with his life. His guilt probably brought him back to Summerville. She started to wonder if that is why he searched her out? Unknowingly, he would take care of the woman whose husband he killed. "Oh, dear God, it's all fitting together now."

She closed her eyes tightly and dragged a pillow over her face to block out the light. Soon sleep returned and took her into another world. She was dreaming about Elgin and the good days. The days with her little girls and loving husband. Everyone was smiling, those were the easy days of her life. She awoke with a smile on her lips until it all came back into focus again. When she realized where she was, she was reduced into a sobbing heap.

The ringing of the phone was relentless now, so she picked it up but didn't speak first.

It was Luke, gasping to speak, "Are you ok, Lilli?"

"I can't talk to you, Luke, I just can't."

She hung up the phone and laid back down on her bed staring at the ceiling fan once again.

Before she knew it, one day turned into a week and a week into a month. She stayed close to home but knew she would have to come out of her shell soon. Her daughters' questioned Luke's disappearance from her life. Lilli would only tell them that things got complicated and they had to work through them if they could. She knew, as the holidays were upon them, that she would have to fess up to Luke being gone.

She had told only her cousin Phyllis the truth about her breaking up with Luke and never wanting to be with him again.

Phyllis told her, "Maybe in time…"

Lilli would always stop her as she tried to talk and said, "There isn't enough time left in my life to forgive, or forget, what he did to Elgin."

She invited the girls over for lunch one afternoon and decided to tell them the whole truth from the first time she met Luke till today. She started by saying that she thought God had sent her a second chance. Another man to love for the last part of her life. She stopped crying because of him and started living once more. She felt young again. Then she told them how good he was to her and always treated her with respect.

"Now comes the hard part. The reason I'm no longer with Luke is because he was the man who ran over your Dad on Hilltop Road. He was drunk and left the scene of the accident. He caused Dad's death but blocked it out for many years. His nightmares got so bad he went to a doctor who put him under sedation with sodium pentothal. It took many weeks, which turned into months, to get this deepest secret out. The secret that caused him nightly terrors and kept him under a dark cloud for too long. "

She confessed, "I'm enduring a second death, of the man I've loved. I miss him, but I know I could never forgive him…even though it was an accident. A life with him would be impossible knowing he took Dad's life away."

Tammy huffed and said, "I didn't trust him because I thought he was cat fishing you for your money. This was never in any realm of reality for me. I'm shocked, I'm mad, and I hate him. Cat fishing would have been a snap, but he's a murderer, I can't even look at him. I never want to see him again."

Jeanne chimed in next, "You are going to call the police? Mom, aren't you? This is a case of vehicular homicide. Does anyone else know about this?"

Lilli said, "Please. Calm down. Only Phyllis knows the truth. My friends just think it ended because we were from two different worlds. Luke has suffered a lot in his own way and I'm not going to have him spend the rest of his lonely life in jail. He has left the club and I haven't accepted his calls in a month. Dad would never want me to put him in jail."

Noelle said, "Nothing will bring back Dad. Why kill another person's life who was obviously an alcoholic and made a tragic mistake? I myself have had one too many glasses of wine and driven home from a girl's night out. It could have been me. He will pay for it the rest of his life. The guilt will eat him up and then losing Mom will surely kill him."

Lilli made them promise not to tell any authorities. It would be too painful for her to go to court and sit through a trial. She would have to relive Elgin's death and then Luke's. She wouldn't survive. Everyone agreed, after many hours of persuasion from Lilli and Noelle. Of course, they would tell their husbands. Lilli asked that they explain to the boys that the only way she can heal is to put it behind her now.

Chapter 31

ONE YEAR LATER

There were now many changes happening around Lilli as her life moved forward. Her poor little companion, Gigi, died and so she was totally alone in the house. Her neighbors, Jenn and Bill, aren't as nosy since their twins Drew and Gianna were born. Lilli actually missed not knowing what was going on in Summerville at warp speed.

The littlest of the children were all now in school. Dana had gotten a promotion at work. Carlton and Noelle bought a bigger house and were loving it. Jeanne and Jamie bought a house on Daniels Island to be closer to his new job. Even though it was further from Lilli, they still visited often. The laughter of the children always shone through even the worst of times. Elgin always believed that change was good to keep you moving forward. Without change you are just standing in one place. "With change, comes growth," was a favorite saying of his.

Lilli and the girls were always afraid of change. Lilli wondered if this fear was instilled in her by her mom. Her mother was born and died in the same house. Just another southern "gift." Lilli thought back when Elgin came home years ago and told her they should move to a farm in the country. The girls all cried, and Lilli said she didn't think it was a great idea. After weeks of tears and pleading he gave up on the idea. Lilli often wondered that maybe if they had moved to the farm, they wouldn't have been on Hilltop Road that night. She thought maybe she could have changed her destiny, Elgin's destiny to be exact.

Now the smells of a 28 lb. turkey in the oven brought back memories of the many Thanksgivings shared in their home. Everyone was together again and smiling. Even though coloring books and markers were set out for the kids, they seemed to enjoy chasing each other around the game room. The laughter made it all bearable.

"Lilli, would you like another glass of wine?" Steve asked.

"No thank you, Steve, I have to finish cooking the meal and then carve the bird."

"I will carve the turkey for you this year, Lilli," Steve lovingly offered.

She admitted she hated carving the turkey. Steve smiled and said he would be honored. He gazed at her with admiring glances throughout the day.

Everyone was now called to the table to enjoy the feast. Of course, there was an empty seat for Elgin. Lilli looked at her table and thought to herself how lucky she was to have all these wonderful people surrounding her. Steve sat next to Lilli and started to dole out the turkey. One could always count on Uncle Steve to be a stable part of the Jackson family. He blended in so easily with her girls, grandbabies, all her sons-in-law and, of course, her. These days, he seems to be the one she turns to for comfort and advice. Her daughters were always hoping he would be the next man in her life.

Small talk at the table continued, but it was mostly about the children and school. Everyone was saying how time was flying by and the kids were all growing up way too fast. Lilli just listened. She thought to herself how she didn't agree time was moving by quickly. Some days still dragged on for her. Most nights were filled with endless thoughts of losses in her life. First, her Mom and Dad, then Lee, Elgin, and yes, even Luke.

Everyone ate and drank way too much for the next few hours. Toasts to everyone who was alive and then to the ones they had lost. After dessert, the adults settled into the living room. The kids returned to the playroom and you could hear them as they enjoyed a game of Simon Says, and the one Lilli taught them from her childhood, red light green light.

It was strange at first for her to see Steve sitting in Elgin's big overstuffed leather chair, but it was funny how she really didn't mind. That chair had been empty far too long. Who better to sit in it than Elgin's best friend?

The girls finished up in the kitchen because it was getting late.

Steve said, "You girls gather up your families and go home, your Mom and I will clean up the kitchen."

The girls smiled and quickly took good old Uncle Steve up on his offer. If it had to be anyone to fill Mom's lonely space, they wanted Uncle Steve. As they kissed their Mom and Steve goodbye, Jeanne leaned over and whispered to him, "Dad is happy you are here taking care of our Mom for him."

Steve gleamed, "I feel the same way."

Gabby and Nicky ran to the car, but not without first shouting out another goodbye to "Grandma and Uncle Steve." Lilli went in first and Steve locked the door behind her.

Steve suggested they finish their wine in the living room before they immerse themselves in the kitchen mess. Lilli smiled and agreed. As they sat in the living room, they watched the last of the votives flickering out.

Steve was still a handsome man with his silver hair and perfect posture. Why couldn't he be the one she fell in love with the second time love came to her? She had become dependent on his dinners at the club and all the social events with the old group. He fits into her past life with Elgin with no effort, no explanations, no defending his honor.

It didn't have to be what it was with Luke. Who needed that intense love that made you sick with fear of not having it forever? With Steve it was easy, like love and life should be with your partner as you are aging. Who needed the drama, the hour long talks and the passionate sex? That was for young people. In your late fifties, you should be with someone that fits like an old shoe.

Steve spoke gently, "Lilli, I have given you enough time to forget

Luke. We have been through many ups and downs in each other's lives for more years than I can now remember. I know we have good times together when we are alone. We have the same friends. We like the same things. I know the girls love me, I fit in here with all of you."

As Lilli looked over at him half surprised, he continued, "Lilli, those are things that most married people don't have and they live happily together for many years. I've loved you my whole life, but I was content watching you, and my best friend go through this world together. I enjoyed being Uncle Steve at all the birthdays, weddings, births and even deaths. I had purpose to my empty life. Then, when you fell for Luke, I thought I would die. I came back in after that to help you recover from that devastating news. I think you are whole again and I don't want to miss out now."

Lilli had no rebuttal because he was right. They did make sense as a couple to fill the lonely dark nights for each other.

She smiled, "Everything you said is right, Steve, but I'm not ready yet. I don't know when I will be ready."

Steve looked at her, "We're not getting any younger, Lilli Belle Jackson. We could surely comfort each other in our golden years." Steve grinned and added, "Just think of this bonus…you will be living with a doctor. Twenty-four, seven, medical aid if you need it."

Lilli giggled and said, "You make a good point there."

They sat quietly and continued to watch the candles dance for them. She could feel the wine settling her down into a sort of trance and memories of Luke swirled around in her head. She was almost ashamed about thinking of him as Steve was professing his love. Steve started talking again but she didn't really hear him.

She couldn't forgive Luke, but she couldn't forget him, either. She didn't want to be stuck like this, but she was. His pleas for forgiveness echoed in her head now. She wanted there to be another car that killed Elgin, but she didn't see it, no one saw it. It was Luke.

Steve realized Lilli was zoning out, so he passed his hand in front of her face, "Earth to Lilli."

They both laughed, and Lilli blamed the wine for making her so spacey. She spoke softly, "I do love you, Steve. Everything you said is one hundred percent true, but I don't know."

"What don't you know Lilli? I've been around you for the last thirty-five years."

Lilli started to list her fears to him, "I don't know if I could love you that way. I don't know if what we have can be sustained. I don't know if I will ever be over the trauma of losing Elgin and then Luke. I just don't' know and don't want to keep you selfishly around. I will admit that you do fit easily into my life. You do make me smile. You do fill my days and nights."

He stopped her, "Those sound like a lot of positives to me, so I will give you as much time as you need. I could never be with anyone else. I'm yours whenever you are ready to have me."

He leaned over and kissed her, and to her surprise, she kissed him back. Lilli was shocked by the kiss as his hands caressed her face and he held her mouth captive longer than she expected. He was strong, but gentle, and Lilli enjoyed his kiss. She thought it must be the wine. Although Steve's conversation and kiss were totally unexpected, they were both exciting to her in a strange way.

Steve told Lilli they better get to the dishes and so they both went into the kitchen. After a while, Steve told her he should leave so she could rest, she had a long day. Lilli smiled and walked him to the door. He told her he would call her tomorrow and maybe they could start Christmas shopping for the kids. She said that would be a great idea.

As she locked the door, she thought that he was still one of the most considerate men she had ever known beside Elgin. How could he have been content standing on the outside of her life and watching her live it with her family for so long?

She thought out loud, "Steve is a wonderful man, why shouldn't I make a life with him? Why should I be alone?" She turned off the lights and walked upstairs.

Lilli then showered, creamed her aging skin, and put on her long cotton pink nightgown. She turned on the television to hear the latest news when the phone rang. She thought it must be one of the girls checking in on her.

Lilli's heart sank as she immediately recognized Luke's voice.

"Hello Lilli, how are you? I was thinking about you and thought how wonderful it would be to hear your voice."

Lilli's words were trapped inside her and as her heart pounded, she answered him in a staccato fashion, "F I N E, LUKE, how are you?"

There was a noticeable silence on the phone and you could hear the pain in his voice as he continued, "I'm surviving. I'm back in Pittsburgh running my Dad's steel mill. My Dad passed away six months ago and I thought I owed it to him to continue his legacy."

She was calmer now, "I'm sorry to hear about your Dad. I know how painful your relationship with him was. It sounds like you made amends with him. I hope it all works out for you."

She wanted this conversation to be over, but didn't know how to end it. She waited patiently for him to speak again.

"Do you go to Mario's anymore? Do you think about us at all? I think about you all the time. I have to know Lilli; will you...will ever forgive me?"

"No, I have never gone back to Mario's. That would be me going back into my past. I must move forward. I forgave you the day I left the cemetery, but I can't forget. When I think about you now, I don't remember all the love we shared or our weekend together on Pawleys Island. I can't remember our many conversations at Mario's either. All I can think of is how you left me on that rainy night up on Hilltop Road."

"I'll never give up trying to get you back in my life Lilli," Luke said remorseful.

The pain of losing Elgin returned and her tone was ice cold, "It's no good Luke, please don't call me again. I'm with Steve now."

She hung up and started to sob. She knew she had just said her final goodbye to the man who was second only to her Elgin. She could have been happy with Luke. She had been so happy with him. As she cried herself to sleep, she vowed it would be the last time she cried for Luke.

THE END?

To my husband Stephen,

"It's not good-bye...it's until I see you again."